MOUNTAIN VIEW

Cover design and typesetting by Geoffrey Bunting
Cover image by Dean Cheng

ISBN 978-1-967756-00-1

First Edition

Published by Otis West
OtisWestBooks.com

Author's Note

This is my first novel—a coming-of-age story set during the summer of 1988. I wrote it in my late twenties while living in San Francisco. For years, the manuscript existed only on a floppy disk, half-forgotten in the back of my desk drawer. It is presented here in its original form—a time capsule from a bygone era.

MOUNTAIN VIEW

A NOVEL

OTIS WEST

One

The sun, which had been lurking behind the administration building all morning, burst suddenly through my dorm room window and beat down on my miserable head. In the hot glare, everything seemed magnified: the whiteness of the walls, the dryness in my throat, the pressure building behind my eyeballs.

Next door, my neighbor had his stereo cranked up to full volume. It was finals week, and Guns N' Roses was a big part of his psych-up routine—he had just started "Welcome to the Jungle" for the third time in a row. I could feel the bass line through the springs in my mattress.

Now that I was awake, all I could think about was water. But getting water required sitting up, required walking. And what I really wanted was this: the coldest, purest water imaginable—spring water, glacier water, water distilled in a test tube and then chilled to the perfect temperature—not the lukewarm, chlorinated stuff that dribbled from the drinking fountain down the hall.

Had I been even slightly less hung over, I might have been happy to realize that this was the last time I would go through this—at least in this bed, in this room. But the fact that I had finished my first year at Berkeley was far from my mind. I was too focused on my thirst, on my head, on fucking Guns N' Roses.

Then the music stopped. I waited for the tape to rewind, for the song to start over again. Instead, my neighbor's door opened and slammed shut.

Other sounds rushed in to fill the void: pigeons cooing on the ledge outside my window, a telephone ringing in the room below, and somewhere, in the distance, a truck backing up, its hazard signal making a steady beep beep beep.

Not exactly peace and quiet, but close. And maybe it was a cloud, or maybe it was the Goodyear blimp moving slowly across the sky, but the sun's intensity seemed to fade a bit. I was starting to drift back to sleep when Gordie burst into the room.

Gordie was my roommate. He was a weird-looking guy—tall and skinny, with bright red hair and a big head. His eyes were too close together, and he had a habit of contorting his face into an odd grimace when he was angry, as he was now.

Gordie grabbed the phone and punched in 9-1-1. He started to say something into the receiver but was put on hold. He looked at me and said, "Someone broke into my truck."

Gordie's father had given him a brand new, bright red Chevy S-10 pickup for high school graduation. Gordie had driven it across the country, not knowing, of course, that Berkeley wasn't Cleveland—he would have to find a place to park the thing. And so he was presented with a choice: pay the University an insane amount to park in one of their official lots, or take his chances on the street. Gordie chose the latter option.

Cars were a liability in Berkeley, a target. Within a few months, Gordie's truck was a mess, with multiple dents, dings and scratches. This wasn't the first break-in, either—there had been several. And two months before, someone had taken a shit in the bed of the truck.

"Yeah police!" he yelled. "My car got broken into. They ripped off my stereo..."

I tried to pull my comforter over my head, but it was snagged on something. I yanked harder and managed to get a corner of it over my ear.

"It's on Dwight. D-W-I... right. Near Bowditch... Okay... When..? Okay."

Gordie hung up.

"I can't believe this. I have a final in two hours."

I said nothing. I was still clinging to my comforter, to the idea of sleep.

"Hey? Think you could come out with me, help me clean up a bit? Wait for the cops to show?"

I didn't answer.

"Come on, Colin. I know you're awake. It's past one o'clock."

I still didn't answer.

"Would you mind?"

"Yes," I said—my voice cracking, my lips and throat dry. "I would mind."

"Great," Gordie said. "That's great. Thanks a lot." Gordie turned and walked out of the room. The door slammed behind him.

It was quiet again, but I was fully awake. I braced myself and then, slowly, eased into a sitting position. My comforter slid off the bare mattress and fell onto a pile of dirty laundry.

My whole head was throbbing now. I could get through this, though. I just had to focus on the task at hand—on getting dressed.

The cuffs of my pants felt wet against my ankles and there was sand in my shoes. I vaguely remembered something about sprinklers and a volleyball court. My t-shirt had a few stains on the front, but I wasn't about to start rummaging around on the floor for another one. Slowly, I walked to the door. I opened it.

Gordie hadn't gotten very far. He was just down the hall, explaining his plight to Julie, a cute sorority girl who seemed to humor him. She had a less good opinion of me, as a result of a small misunderstanding between myself and one of her pledge sisters.

I leaned down and gulped water from the drinking fountain, revolted by the chemical, metallic taste. When I stood upright again, I got a head rush, followed by a wave of nausea. I steadied myself against the wall, then walked toward Gordie.

Gordie turned to me.

"Oh, there's my roommate. So you're going to help me after all?"

I shrugged, tried to smile—for Julie's sake, anyhow.

Julie said, "There's something on your chin."

"A crumb," Gordie said.

"Yeah, or something," Julie said.

Gordie and I were thrown together by a computer. The previous summer, we had filled out some forms detailing our interests and talents and, presto—a perfect match!

The truth was, we were lucky to have housing at all—more than half of the incoming class at Berkeley had to scramble for living arrangements off campus. Gordie and I ended up sharing a cramped room in one of the large residence halls built in the early 70s. And though I'm not sure I would go so far as to say that I actually liked the guy, over the course of the year, I'd grown used to his eccentricities, his habits, his schedule—none of which seemed to collide or grate against my own.

Still, nine months had gone by and I didn't know very much about Gordie. I knew that he was from Cleveland (which I'd had to look up on the map). I knew that his father was some kind of junk mail king—that he made his money buying and selling names. And I knew that Gordie had come west as an act of defiance—his father had wanted him to go to Ohio State, just like everyone else in their family. But beyond that, Gordie never really told me much, and he always got kind of touchy when I tried to ask him anything. He also didn't seem to care to know a whole lot about me. I think he just saw me as a random occurrence, an occasional annoyance, and a potential resource.

For me, coming to Berkeley had been a matter of taking the path of least resistance. I had grown up across the Bay in the not-so-scenic town of Mountain View. I didn't want to stay home and attend community college like many of my friends, but I couldn't conceive of leaving California, either. Six years before, my sister had gone off to UCLA. But I hated Los Angeles—hated the smog and the freeways. Berkeley was close to home, but not too close. I knew people who had come to Berkeley the year before, who liked it. To be honest, my grades in high school weren't all that hot, but I was good at standardized tests—I was good at guessing. Anyway, Berkeley accepted me and so that's where I went.

Gordie had plans. That was obvious the first day we moved in together. He took charge of the room—or his half of it, anyway. There was an order imposed on the desk, on the shelves, that I could never achieve. Books were alphabetized, the bed was always made, and small odds and ends like paper clips and staples, which otherwise would be found rattling around in the bottom of a desk drawer, were corralled into small cardboard boxes and secured by rubber bands. At night, he would diligently floss his teeth while going over his notes from that day's classes.

Gordie wanted to be a doctor, and he fought his way into the prerequisite biology classes. And while I racked up a series of poor grades and incompletes, Gordie built up a nearly perfect academic record. Gordie was determined to work with the famous Dr. Leonard R. Weisman, who had his laboratory at Stanford. With much perseverance, he had landed a summer research job in the Great Man's lab. Gordie was thrilled, but he was too busy and distracted to find a place to live for the summer—which was coming up fast.

I despised people with exotic and interesting summer plans. Sometimes I liked to think that circumstances had conspired against me, but the truth of the matter is, my imagination had failed me, and so once again I was taking the path of least resistance—I was going home to help fix up my father's dilapidated house so he could sell it. It was going to be a dull, boring summer, dealing with my old friends, my father and his stupid girlfriend. And so agreeing to let Gordie stay in my father's broken-down house—knowing that Gordie would probably be dismayed by my father and intimidated by my friends—seemed like a good way to make the summer a little more interesting.

I guess I should admit here that I have always had a strange tendency toward sabotage. Some people might say that I'm simply detached, but I've always suspected something more devious than that. There is something in me that enjoys drama, the slow build-up toward the inevitable.

When we got out to his truck, Gordie, who had relaxed a bit, started muttering to himself and glaring at passersby, as if anyone in the vicinity might be a suspect.

It was a pretty sad sight: the passenger-side window was smashed, the dash was ripped up, and wires were hanging out all over the place. To top it off, someone had tossed a bunch of garbage through the gaping window—a couple of empty beer cans and a half-eaten burrito.

Gordie opened the door and started wiping broken glass off the seat. He was parked right by People's Park, which was filled with dealers and dropouts and drugged-out undergraduates. I guess the People's Park was supposed to be some great idea from the 60s. Last I heard they were going to pave it over, make it into a parking lot or something.

Despite Gordie and his fucked-up truck, there was a festive atmosphere out there. Summer had arrived and school was essentially over. Frat boys were mingling with hippies and girls were rolling around in the grass, giggling.

Gordie finished his clean-up job—shaking out the floor mats, stuffing some of the wires back into the dash. I helped a bit, throwing away the beer cans, picking a few pieces of glass out of the middle of the bench seat. But there wasn't much to do. So then we were just standing there, waiting for the cops.

Gordie was wearing his typical outfit—button-up dress shirt untucked, loose cotton pants and boat shoes. The shirts were always wrinkled—I guess his mom had always ironed them for him. He ended up looking like a rumpled Oxford student.

Gordie started punching his fist into his palm. "Where the hell are they?"

There was always something vaguely accusatory about Gordie's questions. I said, "How should I know?"

I kept blinking—I was having trouble with the glints of sunlight coming off the chrome and windows. Suddenly all I could think of was orange juice. Cold orange juice. I backed away from Gordie and his problems and walked down to the market on the corner.

In the overcrowded aisles of the market, I was overwhelmed by the enticing selection of juices with which to rehydrate myself. I finally selected a large orange juice and walked up front.

I pulled a few crumpled bills from my jeans pockets—happy and somewhat surprised that they were there. The lady behind the counter smoothed them out and got all the presidents facing the same direction before putting them in the register. Suddenly I felt embarrassed, ashamed. I wanted to apologize for being such a slob, but I couldn't seem to form the words. I received my change and walked back into the sunshine, twisting the plastic cap.

The cops had just pulled up. Gordie had a somewhat condescending manner that he lapsed into when he was intimidated or nervous. It was embarrassing to be around him when he was like that, so I kept my distance.

The cops asked some basic questions and filled out their report. Gordie was giving them a hard time—asking them what they were going to do about it—but what could they do? They got back in their car and drove off.

"Pigs," Gordie said.

I leaned against the truck and sucked on my OJ.

Gordie shrugged. "I guess I better get back to studying."

"You gonna be ready to go tonight?"

"I guess so."

"Yeah?" I said. "'Cause I want to get out of here as soon as possible."

Gordie was looking at his truck. "So do I. Believe me."

"Alright. Just make sure you're ready."

"What?" he said. "You want me to skip my final?"

This is what happened sometimes—we'd start bitching at each other like an old married couple. I admit, I was impatient. But I didn't want to be in Berkeley anymore. And the juice wasn't making me feel any better. The orange pulp stuck in my throat.

Gordie just shook his head and looked at his truck.

"Well," I said. "I'll see you tonight."

"Yeah, okay." Gordie looked at his watch. "Jesus."

He turned and started walking away—he had this weird walk, this spring in his step. It was almost like he was skipping or something. I watched him bob down the street.

Two

I had lied to Gordie. I wasn't ready to go yet. I still had to pack. And I had a few loose ends to tie up—I had to pick up my paycheck from the library, and, if I wanted, I could get my final paper from my English composition class. Normally, I wouldn't have been inclined to pick up a paper, but I was pretty sure that I'd failed my other two classes. Maybe I'd get some good news and salvage something from the semester.

The campus was almost empty. Usually, some activist was out in the plaza with a PA system, going off about something or another, but today it was quiet. Just a few people trying to get from point A to point B and some guy throwing a frisbee for his dog.

Earlier in the year I got a job at the Math library. It was the easiest job I ever had. All I had to do was check people's backpacks. If things didn't work out with school, I was thinking of taking that up as a profession.

The Math building was this bunker-type cement thing with ivy climbing up the side. It was always air-conditioned, which created a major vacuum. You had to really lean back and yank just to get the door open, and then you'd practically get sucked in as all the air rushed past you.

Inside, it was quiet. Fred, the janitor, was going over the floor with a big chrome polisher. I had taken a couple of smoke breaks with him (I don't really smoke, but it's a good excuse not to work) and knew more than I wanted to know about his sex life—or sex fantasy life, I was never really sure. He nodded to me. I gave him the thumbs up as I walked past.

I went up to the third floor to find Nelson—my boss. I walked past my post, which was being manned by Josh, a runt of a kid who was supposed to be a calculus champ. It was funny that I had ended up working here. I sucked at math.

As I rounded the corner, I saw Nelson talking to Mrs. Lieberman, this administrator lady who was always chewing on breath mints—you could smell her a mile away. She had him cornered against the card catalog and was hassling him about some new shelving carts that had gone missing.

Nelson was an old gay guy who had been working in the library forever. He had been a helicopter pilot in Korea, and had lost part of his vision when a piece of shrapnel caught him in the temple. When he saw me, his eyebrow—the one with the scar on it—started twitching.

Apparently, Mrs. Lieberman had just finished with him. She huffed and tugged at her dress as she walked away.

Nelson looked at me. "Do I know you?" This was his favorite line. He never got sick of it.

"I want my money," I said.

"Oh you do, do you?"

"Yes," I said, flatly.

Often, Nelson would toy with me further—and there was a second there where he seemed to be considering it—but I think Mrs. Lieberman had knocked the wind out of him. He shrugged and said, "Follow me."

We walked over to his desk, where he pulled out a pack of envelopes. He leafed through them, then handed me mine. Most of the other jobs I'd had over the years had paid me cash under the table. But I liked these official-looking envelopes. I liked seeing my name in that little window.

Nelson said, "Coming back next year?"

"I guess," I said. "I don't know."

He smiled. How many confused undergraduates had he dealt with over the years?

"Have a good summer," he said.

"You, too."

The English building wasn't too far away. It was a big stone building with heavy wooden doors and worn marble steps. There were usually flyers posted all over the doorway, but someone had taken them down. You could still see the neon-colored bits of paper stuck under the leftover staples.

Up on the second floor, some professor lady was gabbing with one of her students, and her kids were crowding the hallway—they had matchbox cars and army men spread out all over the place. I nearly tripped over them as I walked past.

Farther down the hall, a girl was sitting on one of the vinyl benches, crying. I recognized her from one of my classes the previous semester, with her preppy sweater and scuffed-up penny loafers. These were the kind of people I was up against—people who'd cry if they got a bad grade. I stepped past quick, hoping she wouldn't see me.

The papers for my class were all in a box on the floor. I loved that. You paid thousands of dollars to go to school and your papers were thrown in a cardboard box.

I fished my paper out from the bottom. Papers always came back from this TA with a fold down the middle. This had been a big mystery to me—I thought it was some kind of bizarre grading system—until I saw him pedaling across campus on his rusted 3-speed. He folded everything down the middle so he could strap it onto his rack with a bungee cord. Something about that really bothered me.

He'd written a bunch of annoying questions in the margins in pencil—the guy was too wimpy to use a pen. "What do you mean here?" "Is this self-evident?" And my favorite—"Explain?" Then, at the bottom: B.

I hated Bs. Getting a B meant you had tried for an A and failed. I preferred Cs. At least then the teacher knew you didn't give a shit. I stuffed the paper in the trash and walked out.

As I walked back across campus—taking one of those narrow paved walkways that cut across the wide open lawns—I saw Big Jenny walking toward me. There was a point where I could have veered off on another path, but I wasn't up to it. I met her head on.

Big Jenny was this girl I'd met during a brief stint at the radio station. She was six feet tall and skinny. Usually she had this chubby girl sidekick—they were like Abbott and Costello—but she wasn't around. Big Jenny was a major power freak at the station. She was always trying to boss me around, trying to get me to do shit work like clean out a closet or lick stamps. I didn't last long.

Her hair was dyed black and she wore too much black eyeliner. She looked bored and unimpressed.

"Colin," she said. "Colin, Colin, Colin, Colin."

"Jenny, Jenny, Jenny."

"What are you up to?"

"Just got my paycheck." I waved it as proof.

She nodded. She was wearing this funky outfit—this too-small plaid sweater, a skirt and big boots.

"Is that your cheerleader getup?" I said.

She snorted. "So funny."

I was waiting for some sort of witty retort—something about what an idiot I was—but it didn't come.

"Well, hey," I said. "Have a good summer."

"You too," she said. Then, "Doing anything exciting?"

"Nope," I said. "Just going home. You?"

"I'm going to Greece."

"Oh yeah?" I said.

"Yeah, I'm going to be working on an archeological dig."

"Great," I said. "That's great." I started backing away. "Have a great time."

What the hell was she gonna do on an archeological dig? I couldn't see her actually digging, or doing any real work for that matter. She'd probably try to boss people around—try to make them fetch cold drinks or something.

So now all I really had to do was pack. But I didn't want to go back to the room and get stuck talking to people, saying a bunch of fake good-byes, etc.

I decided to go check on Pablo. I couldn't remember exactly how we'd left off the night before. We'd gotten into an argument—I was still trying to remember exactly how it had started and what it had even been about.

Pablo and I had met in a huge registration line at the beginning of the year. He had grown up in Fremont—across the Bay from Mountain View and just south of Berkeley.

For the past month or two, Pablo had been living with his sister. He had been all set in a fairly decent apartment off Shattuck Street until a few months back, when the guy who lived in the apartment below him fell asleep with a cigarette burning and set his bed on fire. The fire department got there pretty quick, but not before the flames burned a hole through the ceiling—Pablo's floor—and took out most of Pablo's room. Everything that didn't burn got melted. Afterwards, his mini refrigerator looked like a huge, melted ice-cream sandwich.

Pablo's sister was about four years older and in a Biochemistry master's program at Berkeley. Pablo's arrangement at her place was only temporary—he was to stay until the year was up, at which point he was moving to San Francisco for some kind of internship. I didn't get the deal with internships—the whole concept of it bugged me. Working for free. But then Pablo had gone ahead and made some basic assumptions about life and jobs that I had failed to make.

I had a bit of a walk ahead of me—Pablo's sister lived in a residential area about a mile from campus. But the walk would be good for me. It would help to work all the poison out of my system. As I walked down the tree-lined streets, I started to remember the previous evening.

After Pablo and I finished our last final, we started drinking to celebrate—first at my dorm, then at some stupid frat party. Then, many hours later, we ended up at this art student's apartment. Some guy had taken a Super-8 camera and filmed a porno flick while it was playing on his shitty little TV, which gave it this low-tech, black and white grainy effect. So now there were a bunch of guys standing around, watching a porno flick with the pretense that it was art. It was the stupidest thing I had ever seen. I was pretty drunk by then and I made a few comments, which people seemed to ignore. I don't think Pablo really had an opinion one way or the other, but after we left, he started fucking with me about it, playing devil's advocate.

Then, somehow, the argument mutated and got personal. I had lost the thread, but suddenly I was being tried on a technicality. Suddenly Pablo was calling me a prude. He said I was too judgmental, that I took shit too seriously. I got defensive—saying that what had pissed me off was the fact that these guys were so full of themselves, not the sex or "degradation of women" or whatever—all the while suspecting that he was right.

And that's when we stumbled onto a volleyball court with a bunch of naked people. They were hanging out in the sand on lawn chairs like they were at the beach. Then the sprinklers came on.

The whole thing seemed perfectly timed with our argument, almost staged. So we were just standing there, with all these hippies—future stockbrokers, dentists and accountants—running around naked in the sprinklers, daring us to join them. Pablo thought the whole thing was hilarious—he was laughing at the hippies, laughing at me. Then he started taking his clothes off, too—laughing and falling over as he tried to get his shoes and pants off.

I don't know, maybe I am a prude. Fuck it. I walked home by myself.

Three

Pablo's sister lived in a three-story apartment complex. Next door, some guy was washing his Mustang, and soapy water was running across the sidewalk and into the street. By the time I reached the front gate, my sloppy wet footprints had faded into the distinct crisscross patterns of my Chuck Taylors.

I climbed the cement steps to the second floor and knocked. I knocked again. Then I tried the door. It was open.

Pablo was sitting on the couch with a light focused on his leg. He was poking at his skin with a safety pin.

"What are you doing?" I said.

He looked up at me, then back at his leg. "I think I fell in a bush on the way home last night. I got this big ol' splinter in my leg."

Pablo had recently cut his hair short, and he had a cowlick that looked like a crop circle—like aliens had landed on his head. He was wearing shorts and an old Cal sweatshirt with bleach stains on the front.

Pablo was wincing. "Fuck," he said. "This hurts like shit."

I leaned against the kitchenette counter. His sister's tiny dog—Shelly—was cowering by its food bowl. The dog hated me. It was like a tiny Doberman, but with everything shrunk down except the eyes, which kind of bugged out at you.

I said, "Tell Shelly to relax."

"Shelly, relax."

The dog flattened its ears and backed away, keeping its eyes on me the whole time.

"How you feeling?" I said.

"Fine, 'cept for this friggin' splinter. You?"

"Okay, now."

"Feels good to be done, doesn't it?"

"I guess." I picked up a Vogue and started flipping through it. His sister always had tons of magazines lying around. Since Pablo had started living with her, we had both accumulated a bunch of useless fashion and enter-tainment knowledge.

"I found a place in SF," Pablo said.

"Yeah?"

"Yeah, the guy sounds like a freak. But it's cheap, and it's only for three months, so what the fuck, right?"

"Sounds good to me," I said. I decided that Pablo had temporarily forgotten about the whole thing with the porn video and the hippies on the volleyball court—other-wise, he would have started in on me by now.

Then I said, "Gordie's truck got busted into again."

Pablo started laughing. He hated Gordie.

"That fucker. I bet he was freaking."

"Pretty much," I said. "I don't know. I felt kind of sorry for him."

"Yeah, I feel sorry for him, too. Poor Gordie."

I kept flipping through the magazine, which wafted toxic-smelling perfume in my face. I still felt vaguely ill, still had this bad chemical feeling—my skin felt kind of prickly, and the blood seemed to be swirling around awfully close to the surface. So I wasn't really listening when Pablo launched into a story about the time he got chickenpox.

The truth is, I didn't have to listen—I could get the whole picture from one detail. Sometimes, it was almost like we spoke in code. He'd just say, "It was like... you know?" And usually I did. It was frightening how much we had in common, how much shared experience we had—and what a fucking cliché most of it was. One of us would be in the middle of some stupid story about our childhood—how we blew up model cars with M-80s or how we got busted for shoplifting Jolly Ranchers when we were eight, and it would be like, "You did that, too?"

Still, I sometimes felt weird hanging out with Pablo. He was so mellow, so at ease with himself, at ease with the world. That's what I liked about him, and that's also what made me vaguely envious. I mean, I did a decent job of acting mellow, acting cool, but sometimes I felt like I had more in common with the uptight Gordie.

There was the sound of keys at the door. The door opened, and Pablo's sister walked in.

Anne. She was a knockout. And she didn't exactly pull her punches, either. She was wearing tight shorts and an equally form-fitting tank top. I tried not to stare.

She put her keys on the counter. "Hi Colin," she said. Then, "Pablo, I told you to keep the door locked."

"Yeah, yeah."

She went to the fridge and pulled out a mason jar filled with water. She unscrewed the lid and poured herself a glass. "Any calls?"

Pablo said, "Nope."

Anne frowned when she saw Pablo digging at his leg with the safety pin. "What are you doing?" Then she said, "Actually, I don't want to know."

At this point, the dog reappeared and started working itself into a frenzy. Its tiny body was shaking with excitement.

Anne went into baby-talk mode. "Hello sweetie," she said. "Oh, you want your walkie, don't you?"

When she took the leash out of the cupboard, the dog went apeshit. It started prancing back and forth on the linoleum, its little toenails like miniature tap shoes.

"Well, I have to pee first. Then I'll take you." She handed me the leash. "Could you hold this a second?" She disappeared down the hall.

When the dog saw that I had the leash, it flattened its ears back and sat down.

Pablo gave up on the splinter. He tossed the safety pin on the coffee table. "Fuck it." Then he said, "You hungry?"

"A bit."

Pablo walked over to the fridge. He opened it and started shaking his head. "All she ever buys is diet shit."

He pulled out a yogurt. "Check this out. It's chock-full of Aspartame. That shit will kill you." He put back the yogurt and pulled out some celery. "She read somewhere that you actually burn more calories chewing this than you gain by eating it."

I'd heard this whole harangue before. Living with his sister had turned him into a reactionary nutritionist.

Anne re-appeared and relieved me of the leash. "Thank you."

Pablo waved the celery in the air. "Why don't you buy some real food for once?"

"Buy your own damn food." Anne bent down and attached the leash to the dog's collar. Again, I tried not to stare.

"Let's go Shelly." She opened the front door. "See you guys."

"Bye," I said. I watched her go out the door.

Pablo put the celery back in the fridge. "We could go over to Satyricon."

"We could," I said. Satyricon was a nearby co-op—it had been a frat house until the 60s, when it got taken over by hippies. Pablo pretended that he was friends with a few of them in order to get a free meal every once in a while.

"Let's do it." Pablo felt around in his pockets. "Keys. Where are my keys?"

As we were walking out front, Mercedes Steve pulled up across the street in his silver 280 SEL.

Mercedes Steve was Anne's latest boyfriend. He was a med student with lots of family money behind him. Pablo and I had started calling him Mercedes Steve to differentiate him from another of Anne's suitors named Steve—a mild-mannered engineering student who drove a Civic.

The power windows came down. There he was, in the splendor of wood and red leather. He had a sweater tied around his neck and sunglasses pushed back over his greasy hair. He looked like a preppy rock star.

I saw then that there was a girl sitting in the passenger seat, someone I had never seen before.

Mercedes Steve said, "Your sister around?"

Pablo shrugged casually, trying to play it cool in front of the girl. "She's walking the pooch."

"So she'll be back soon?"

"I'd guess so."

He looked at me. "Hey Colin."

"How you doing?"

He nodded importantly. "Good." Then he decided to make the introduction. "This is my sister, Chloe."

We all said hi. His sister was pretty amazing, with long brown hair and green eyes.

A couple of seconds went by. Then Pablo said, "We're gonna go get some food."

"Alright. Take it easy."

"You too."

We started walking. After a moment, I said, "I didn't know Mercedes Steve had a sister."

"I knew," he said. "I just didn't know she looked like that."

I could see the wheels turning. Pablo didn't look too happy, though. His sister's boyfriend's sister—that was too incestuous, even for Pablo.

We walked past an old Impala up on blocks and then alongside a fenced-in school yard where some kids were playing baseball with an aluminum bat and a tennis ball. Pablo stopped to watch.

The kid at bat kept letting balls go by. The ball would bounce against the wall behind him, he would turn to pick it up, then toss it lazily back to the pitcher. The outfielders looked bored.

When the kid let another one go by, Pablo cupped his hands around his mouth and yelled, "Tell the fucker to swing!"

The kids turned to look at us, squinting against the dull glare of the low sun.

The kid at bat said, "What'd he say?"

Pablo laughed and again yelled, "Swing! Tell him to swing!"

The pitcher looked back at the kid and shrugged. Then he pitched the ball.

The kid swung and missed.

Satyricon was wedged between two legitimate frat houses. It looked about the same as the others, except for its Rastafarian paint scheme. Once, I'd seen a couple of older guys standing out front in their dress shirts and loafers, trying to figure out what had happened to their old frat house. They'd seemed angry.

As we walked up, a guy with a shaved head was carrying a lamp out to his Toyota hatchback, which was sagging under the weight of a futon and a million books. A small orange kitten chased and continually pounced on the electrical cord as it skipped down the front walkway.

It was dark and cool inside, kind of like a church. Only there was that stale smell. A lot of beer had been spilled on the carpet. A lot of other stuff, too.

There were a few hippie-types milling around in the kitchen. A dog with a bandanna tied around its neck was licking what looked like spaghetti sauce off the table. Pablo ignored everyone and went straight over to the industrial-size fridge. He opened it and pulled out a huge vat of mayonnaise and some grayish roast beef. He found some bread.

"Want a sandwich?"

I said, "No thanks." I had lost my appetite.

I sat down at the big table and watched. Pablo unscrewed the top of the mayo, frowned, then reached into the vat with his hand.

"Someone missing some photos?"

He plopped a couple of mayo-smeared photographs on the table.

The hippies crowded around to admire the display. They were laughing.

"Is that Eric?"

"I think so."

"No, that's not Eric."

"Well, who is it?"

I felt tired. I stood up, walked out of the kitchen and went and sat on one of the old brown vinyl couches in the main room. The room was empty, aside from a big color TV and a pool table with torn-up felt. There were a couple of broken pool cues in the corner.

Two lesbians were playing checkers by the window, with their matching bomber jackets and crewcuts. I'd seen them do this before—I wasn't sure if they were actually playing or if it was just for show.

I sank back into the couch. I could see myself reflected in the gray-green screen of the television. I closed my eyes.

I was starting to think about home, about the summer ahead of me. I was ready to get out of Berkeley, but I wasn't sure I was ready to go back home, to deal with my father. My best friend Jack would be around, but we didn't seem to have much to say to each other anymore. And then there was Beth, too, though I didn't know if she'd be back home for the summer or not. I couldn't decide if I cared, either.

I opened my eyes. One of the lesbians said, "Pablo said to tell you he'd be right back."

I nodded, closed my eyes again. This time I was thinking about that girl, Mercedes Steve's sister, Chloe. Those green eyes.

When I woke up, the lesbians were gone. Two scruffy-looking guys were standing in front of the TV, kind of looking around. When they saw that I was awake, one of them said, "Hey, man, how's it going?"

"Fine," I said.

"We're supposed to repair this."

"Alright," I said.

"Yeah," the other guy said. "We got a call."

"Sure," I said.

They looked at each other, then started to lift. It was a pretty big TV.

"Hey buddy, think you could get the door for us?"

I shrugged, then got up and opened the door.

"Thanks. We really appreciate that, man."

I watched the two thieves take the TV out to their beat-up van. They got in and drove away.

It was getting dark. Where the fuck was Pablo?

While I was standing there, a red BMW pulled up in front of the house, and a beautiful blond girl got out with two people who looked like her parents. They walked up the front steps. The girl smiled and said, "Hi."

"Hi," I said.

"These are my parents."

"Nice to meet you," I said.

The parents nodded and smiled.

"Have you seen Shelly?"

"Shelly the dog?"

She looked confused. "No. Shelly the person."

"I haven't seen her," I said.

"Thanks." She smiled. Her parents smiled, too, and they all entered the house.

Just then, the streetlights flared to life—first turning chalky white, then glowing into a deeper yellow-orange.

I looked at my watch. It was almost eight o'clock. Gordie would be done with his final soon. It was time to go back and pack.

Four

Packing was easy. There was nothing to it, really. It was just throwing clothes into trash bags.

I didn't have that much stuff to begin with. I wasn't one of those people who got really into decorating their room. Some people had set up their rooms with these elaborate themes, like the girl down the hall with the pink teddy bears—pink teddy bear sheets, pink teddy bear towels, pink teddy bear posters, etc. And then there were the people who went for a radical change—a new start, a new persona. This strategy could backfire, like the kid who showed up as a "mod"—only, he got the shoes wrong, and some of the band posters weren't quite right. The "real" mods persecuted the shit out of him. People are mean like that. They don't cut you any slack.

My room back home in Mountain View was a trash heap—I wasn't going to haul all my junk over to Berkeley. I just brought some clothes and a few tapes. I was actually proud of the fact that there was nothing on my dorm room wall.

Gordie hadn't done much either, besides be neat as hell. All he had was a debate team trophy from high school and a poster of Einstein. That poster was plenty, though. Earlier in the year, I had this political girlfriend, and when she saw that poster, she started giving Gordie a ton of grief about the Manhattan Project. They got in a huge fight about it.

Anyway, I didn't have too much stuff, but there was still a ton of crap to throw out. Mostly it was junk like class schedules, handouts and flyers for various events I never seemed to make it to. Then there were photos of people I hadn't seen since the first month of school, and clothing I didn't recognize. I found some girl's hair clip under my bed—I remember how she had sworn up and down that she had left it in our room, and how I had sworn up and down that she hadn't. I tossed it out.

So it took a bit longer than I expected, but I still managed to get it under control. Luckily, I'd sold back all my books the week before when I was low on cash. So after hauling a bunch of garbage downstairs, I was left with just two trash bags of clothes and a few odds and ends which I threw into a duffel bag.

The last thing I found was my hand-held electronic football game. I'd gotten it for Christmas when I was a kid. I must have tossed the game in randomly when I was packing at home, and then it got buried in a drawer almost immediately. The battery cover was held on by duct tape and the reverse button was broken, but you could still play just fine.

There were two levels: Pro 1 and Pro 2. It was pretty hard to play Pro 2 without the reverse button, but I was mostly into Pro 1 anyway, not because I couldn't hack the faster speed of Pro 2, but because Pro 1 was kind of relaxing. I'd get the defense going one way, and then I was gone, my little red dot—which was brighter than the defense's little red dots—just cruising down the sideline, racking up the big points. A cheesy little victory tune would play when you scored a touchdown, and then I'd do it over again, playing for the opposite team. So it was usually a tied score at the end of the game, like 98 to 98, unless the time ran out and one team won by a touchdown, like 112 to 105.

I was playing when Pablo came in.

"Man, where the fuck did you go?"

"Where did you go?" I said.

"I was upstairs. Didn't those chicks tell you?"

"They said to wait."

"No, that was before. Then I told them to tell you I was upstairs."

"I didn't get the message."

"Whatever."

Pablo sat on Gordie's bed. Anytime Gordie came in, he would look really stressed if Pablo was sitting on his bed. Pablo knew it and did it on purpose.

"Hey," Pablo said. "So I was just in Joey's room. They ordered a pizza."

"Yeah?"

Joey lived directly below us. He was from Hawaii, and his brother express-mailed him pot every two weeks.

"Yeah, and Linda's there. She said she's been looking for you."

"Oh, great."

Pablo looked around. "You done packing?"

"I guess."

"Where's the roommate?"

"Fuck if I know. We're supposed to be out of here."

"Come hang out a while."

"Yeah, alright."

"Well, come on."

"You go down. I'll be there in a second."

"Alright. But you better come down."

"I will."

As soon as Pablo left, I started on the game again. It was the fourth quarter, just 7:13 left. It was tied, 84 to 84.

Linda was that political girl who got all freaky about Gordie's Einstein poster. She got freaky about lots of stuff. She was always involved in the various demonstrations that are a fixture at Berkeley, and she seemed disappointed that I wasn't interested in picketing nuclear power plants or spiking trees. But that's not why we broke up. Not the main reason, anyway.

We were together for a good part of the first semester. I even went down and met her folks in Pasadena when Cal was playing UCLA in football. Her dad was a UCLA alum, and he kept trying to get a rise out of me when UCLA won—like I could give a shit about football. The dad was a doctor. It was a whole family of achievers, which was part of the problem. I can't talk about what I'm going to do all the time. Linda was into that—her plans. And I'm sure she's going to do all that stuff—work for peace and the environment or something.

But what really freaked me out was the whole molding thing. Some couples get really into it—you'll see them start wearing the same clothes, they start doing the same things all the time, and they get into this stupid baby-talk routine. I hate that—it makes me want to puke. I could see that Linda was trying to steer us into that mode. She started buying me clothes—first a Che Guevara beret, then an army surplus jacket. Plus, she always wanted us to have the same opinions about things. If we ever disagreed about something—even something stupid like where to eat or what movie to see—she'd get really concerned and we'd have to talk it out until we found some kind of middle ground.

So after a while, I started avoiding her. And whenever we were together, I acted sad and depressed. But that just made it worse—it made her feel sorry for me and want to help me. The truth of the matter was, I WAS sad and depressed. And it wasn't just Linda, either—it was everything. For the most part, I had no idea what the fuck I was doing at college—but I didn't know what else I should be doing, either. Anyway, I stuck to my act, and after a while she gave up on me.

Linda was the only girlfriend I'd had at Berkeley (and only the second girl I'd slept with during the year—there had been a drunk and humiliating night in the second week with this weird punk rock girl two floors above me—a floor I avoided for the rest of the year). So after Linda, I decided to stay away from girls for a while. One night, while drinking heavily with Pablo, I even went so far as to make a vow of celibacy. Pablo thought it was hilarious. He started calling me a monk, then monkey boy.

But here's the thing: I was starting to realize I was negative all the time—a spoilsport and judgmental as hell about everything and everybody. What was wrong with me? One time, after I made a sarcastic comment about student government, Linda called me a nihilist. She'd been reading Nietzsche for a class, and I think she meant it as a compliment, but still, it bummed me out. I think Berkeley was just crowding in on me too much. I knew that I needed to step back from everything and take a deep breath.

Joey always kept his door shut with a towel wedged under it—mostly because a bunch of the Reagan youth in his hall disliked his pot smoking. Also, he was kind of paranoid.

So the door got stuck when I tried to open it. There was all this, "Who is it? Hold on a second," and then the door opened and Joey was there with a big stupid grin on his face. He was a tall skinny guy with his blonde hair already thinning.

Joey said, "Dude, Colin, what's up?" He had this stupid handshake you always had to do with him. Typical pot smoker. Behind him were Linda and Pablo and this girl whose name I could never remember—Pablo had slept with her the first week of school.

Pablo said, "It's the man himself!"

"Hi Colin," Linda said. She smiled. She looked good. She always had this healthy glow. And she was obviously wasted. That just made her more sincere.

The other girl was fiddling with this ridiculously large bong made out of glass tubes and copper piping. It looked like a high school science project.

"Dude, have a seat."

I sat down on the floor. Joey's roommate was never around. He was this little Armenian kid, and he hated Joey. His family lived nearby, and he seemed to spend most of his time there, hiding. His side of the room was decorated with all these religious items—gold elephants and colorful crosses—which everyone thought were really cool. In a way, I think Joey was proud of them.

The girl offered me the bong. I said no thanks.

"Give it to me then," Pablo said.

Linda said, "So Pablo says you're all packed up."

"Yup."

"That's great." She was just kind of smiling at me. It made me uncomfortable. "What are you going to do this summer?"

"I'm going to Greece."

"Really?" Linda said.

"Yeah, I'm going to be working on an archeological dig."

Pablo choked and a bunch of pot smoke came out of his nose. He gave me a look.

"That sounds really fantastic," Linda said. "I'm glad you found something you're interested in."

"Oh yeah," I said.

"Dude's gonna dig up some mummies and shit," Pablo said. He laughed, and more smoke came out of his nose.

"Mummies?" Linda said.

"No," I said. "You know, pottery and stuff."

"Oh," Linda said.

"I know someone who did that," Joey said.

That's when I felt it—I wiped at my nose and came back with blood on my fingers.

"You okay?" Linda said.

"I'll be right back."

I walked down the hall to the bathroom. I went into one of the stalls, got a huge wad of toilet paper, stuffed it against my nose and sat down. I leaned way back.

I'd had quite a few bloody noses since I'd started Berkeley. It was getting so that I was used to them. I'd had one while reading in the library—blood dripping right onto the pages of The Great Gatsby before I knew what was happening. I closed the book and shelved it—leaving a bloody Rorschach where Daisy starts crying over Gatsby's shirts.

I heard someone come into the bathroom. Whoever it was walked into the stall next to me. I heard him tear off the toilet seat protection thing and sit down. He cleared his throat and then started humming.

I checked the wad of toilet paper, which had soaked through. Fresh blood is very red—so very red against white toilet paper. But the bleeding had stopped.

I went to the sink and cleaned up—washing my hands and carefully washing my face. I looked at myself in the mirror. I was pale as hell. Sometimes I felt like a fucking Romanov.

The pizza arrived just as I got back. There was a big argument over whether or not the delivery guy had made it on time, and whether or not he owed us the pizza for free because he was late. The poor guy had to call his manager.

For a campus filled with a bunch of supposed liberals, there sure was a lot of abuse of the working man. Finally, when it became clear that the pizza was going to come out of the guy's paycheck, everyone agreed to pay up.

After the delivery guy left, there was controversy over what Joey had ordered—Linda was allergic to mushrooms and the other girl didn't eat red meat. That pizza got picked to death. Anyway, it didn't seem like it, but I was there for a long time—all of a sudden it was almost midnight. I decided to call up to the room. As I was dialing, it occurred to me that we hadn't disconnected the phone.

Gordie answered. "Did you just call and hang up?"

"No," I said.

There was a silence at the other end of the line.

"Hello?" I said.

"Where the hell are you? I thought we were leaving."

"We are," I said. "I'll be up there in a minute."

"Alright."

"We gotta disconnect the phone."

"What?"

"The phone. We have to disconnect it."

"Oh yeah."

"I'll be up."

"Yeah," he said. "Okay."

I hung up and looked at Pablo. "I gotta go."

"Alright."

Linda was dozing off—she'd wake up from time to time and smile. Joey and the other girl were slumped against each other, humming along with some reggae record Joey had put on the turntable.

I stood up. "Bye," I said.

"Oh," Linda said. "Bye." She got up and gave me a big hug. "Take care of yourself."

"You too," I said.

Pablo stood up, too. "I'm gonna jet."

"I guess I better go, too," Linda said. We all turned and said good-bye to Joey and the other girl, but they were too out of it to notice.

Linda and I said good-bye again in the hallway. She gave me another hug.

Pablo said, "I'm coming with you. I gotta say good-bye to your roomie."

"Alright," I said. "You can help us carry shit out to the truck."

"Oh great," Pablo said.

Gordie was pacing around the room.

"How was the final?" I said.

"Bad." He glanced at Pablo.

Pablo said, "Hey buddy. How's my buddy?"

Gordie looked annoyed.

"Pablo's gonna help us out."

"Fine," Gordie said.

Gordie's bedding was folded up and his books were packed away in boxes. His two suitcases—which had waited patiently under his bed for nine months—were packed and ready to go.

Pablo picked up Gordie's debate team trophy, which was sitting in an open box on the desk. Pablo had stolen it from Gordie a couple of times. He liked to bring it to parties.

"Can I have this?" Pablo said. "Seriously. It's very... special."

"Give me that," Gordie said, and snatched it away. He put it back in the box.

Then I saw the flashing green light on the answering machine.

"We have a message," I said.

"Oh yeah," Gordie said.

I hit PLAY, and my mother's voice flowed into the room.

"Hi Colin. This is your mother just calling to say that I'm thinking of you."

I could see her in her air-conditioned office in Phoenix, talking on the speaker phone. She had one of those desks with glass on top, and a bunch of real estate awards framed on the walls.

"I hope your finals went well. If you don't get a chance to call before you go, give me a call when you get home. I love you. Hi to Gordie. Okay. Bye."

When she hung up, Pablo smirked. "Cool mom."

I said, "Shut up," and hit ERASE. Then I unplugged the machine and tossed it into Gordie's box.

"Ready?" Gordie said.

"Let's do it," I said.

It took us three trips to load up the truck. After the first trip, Gordie stayed with the truck to guard the stuff.

As Pablo and I walked back to the dorm, Pablo said, "How come he gets to stay with the truck?"

"You can next time."

"No," Pablo said. "That's okay."

On the last trip down—after giving a last look around my room, which still had some trash, but fuck it—I lost Pablo. He had taken Gordie's box of books, but when I got to the truck, he was no longer with me.

Gordie was all pissed off. "Where the hell is he?"

"He was right behind me."

I looked around. It was quiet. Lights were still on in most of the dorm rooms.

"I can't believe you're friends with that guy."

I shrugged.

Finally, Pablo appeared. He had this girl with him. He dumped the box of books in the back of the truck. Then he came around to shake my hand.

"Colin, man. Take it easy."

"I will."

"You're gonna come visit me in SF, right?"

"Hell yeah."

"Oh, this is Cindy."

Cindy said hi.

"Are we going or what?" Gordie said.

"Bye Gordie!" Pablo said. "You're welcome for all the help."

"Whatever," Gordie mumbled. He started the truck.

"Give me a call from your new place," I said.

"I will."

We pulled away. I looked in the rear-view mirror. Pablo was walking away with his arm around the girl.

For *The Graduate*, they wanted a shot of Dustin Hoffman driving his red Alfa Romeo across the Bay Bridge toward Berkeley. The problem is, that would have put him on the lower deck, which is dark and not very dramatic. So they showed him driving on the top deck—even though people from the Bay Area would know that he was going in the wrong direction.

But I can see why they did it. Because when you're on the top deck, driving toward San Francisco, and you emerge from the tunnel that goes through Treasure Island—well, there's nothing quite like it. Of course, they couldn't show you the best view of all—of San Francisco looming up before you with all its lights.

I was kind of glad they'd stolen Gordie's stereo. Otherwise, he would have been playing one of his stupid King Crimson tapes, which would have spoiled the mood. So it was nice and quiet, except for the wind rushing through the busted window. Mist swirled around the bridge's huge steel towers. I was only forty minutes from home.

Five

I woke up early because the guy next door got the great idea to fire up his leaf blower. It was about eight o'clock. I had slept maybe five hours.

I got up and walked out back. Our yard was a mess of dirt and crabgrass—my father hadn't been watering, either out of laziness or out of respect for the drought. There were several knee-high weeds growing quite well, though. They must have had deep roots.

The guy had just finished blowing all the dust and leaves off his patio and was already stashing the thing back in his little potting shed. He was a short yuppie guy who had moved in right before I left for Berkeley. Over the course of the year, he had built a Jacuzzi and turned his backyard into a sculpture garden—mermaids and cherubs and gargoyles facing each other across a perfectly green lawn. I glared at him over the fence for a while, but the guy was oblivious. I walked back inside.

The night before, Gordie and I had to break into the house—climbing through a small bathroom window and knocking over my father's various shampoo and medicine bottles. The house had been dark and quiet—the stillness broken only by the faint blinking of the VCR's digital clock.

My father had started using my room for storage, and I stumbled over a pile of boxes when I walked in. I slept in my old sleeping bag on my bare mattress. Gordie slept on the living room couch under some blankets I'd taken from my father's room. Eventually, I'd put him in my sister's old room, but at the moment it was piled too high with crap.

Gordie was still asleep, breathing deeply, his face pressed into the vinyl seat cushion. There was a nice little puddle of drool under his chin.

The kitchen sink was filled with dirty dishes. My father's prescription sunglasses sat on the counter beside an uncapped aspirin bottle. As I went to open the refrigerator, I was confronted by a photo of my father's girlfriend, held in place by a small, lemon-shaped magnet. The woman—Gwen—was smiling and wearing a hat with fake flowers on it. She taught art at my old junior high school and painted huge wall-sized paintings from postcards. There was one hanging in the living room—the Pantheon done in pinks and purples.

When I opened the refrigerator, I found some leftover chicken, mashed potatoes and a carton of milk. The milk was spoiled.

I boiled water for coffee, only to find there weren't any paper filters. I made tea and found some stale bread for toast.

And then I noticed the kitchen table. It was brand new—a cheap folding table with a vinyl top. My father and I had always eaten in the living room or standing up at the kitchen counter. As I sat down with the tea and toast, I realized that I hadn't sat down to breakfast in our house since before my mother moved out.

Our house was an Eichler—part of the housing explosion in the South Bay in the 1950s. It had sliding glass doors, giant plate glass windows and plywood walls, and when my family moved here from Denver, it seemed like a futuristic dream house—all that glass, all that California sunshine. But there was a lot of overhang from the roof, and the property wasn't all that big—the fence was very close on both sides. And so the house stayed dark in the winter—and cold. When it rained, water trailed off the flat roof and rattled the gravel walkway that circled our house. The bottom two feet of glass were covered by a green-brown algae, like the inside of an aquarium.

My parents got divorced a year after my sister went off to college. My mother took much of the furniture with her, and the house remained relatively empty and became increasingly run down. My father quit his job at Hewlett-Packard and started his own business, and the living room was soon filled with dismantled computer equipment. He divided all of his money between his business and alimony, so there was nothing left to maintain the house. We lived with the leaks in the roof, the loose tiles in the bathroom, the windows that were stuck either open or closed.

My father eventually turned to consulting—putting aside his ideas to help others with theirs—and as he began to travel more, the house became my domain. Then he met Gwen and started spending more and more time with her—first at her place, then at the new condo they had purchased together. So I was having trouble adjusting to the idea that my father was selling what I had long considered to be my house.

When I finished breakfast, I did the dishes and wiped off the counter. There wasn't any liquid soap, but I found some Comet under the sink, which of course made me sing, "Comet, it makes you vomit!" That done, I decided to look around the house.

My father's room was a mess of clothes, cardboard boxes and paper bags filled with garbage. There was a pile of bills on his dresser, along with several real estate pamphlets. I flipped through these, looking at photos of houses—each coupled with brief descriptions and smaller, underexposed interior shots. I imagined our house being presented as a "fixer-upper," with its weed garden, cracked patio and loose-hinged doors.

I walked out to the garage, which was crammed full of junk—a car hadn't been parked in there for years. Crap was stacked up against the only window, and it was dark as hell. I pulled the string for the light, but the filament popped. Slowly, my eyes adjusted.

Aside from the stacks of computer equipment, there were rusted skis, old tires, tennis rackets, mildewed rugs, my old Big Wheel and a lawnmower with a cracked cylinder block. As I maneuvered around toward the side door, I found a chipped mug with my mother's face on it—a photo image from an amusement park outside my grandparents' house in San Diego. I remembered this trip only vaguely—my sister losing her hat on the water ride, and a particularly fierce argument between my parents in a Denny's. The mug held the powdered remains of coffee, and a dead fly.

Outside, the sun was hot on our driveway. Gordie's pickup was parked there with its broken window and a bunch of our stuff still in the back. I could hear the wind chimes on the old widow's porch next door.

Some kids were circling around on BMX bikes, making skid marks on the sidewalk and doing jumps off a plywood ramp. One kid was sitting on the curb with a cast on his arm, watching his friends.

I was suddenly confused. Was it the weekend? Or was school out? When I asked the kid with the cast what day it was, he looked at me like I was insane.

"It's Saturday," he said.

I turned and looked at Jack's house, directly across the street. His father's little Datsun was parked out front, the dented hubcaps glistening in the sun. I stepped off the sidewalk and crossed the street.

I opened the Patricks' front door and walked in. I was greeted by the dogs. They had four golden retrievers, and Jesse, the largest, almost knocked me down.

The Patricks' house was always slightly warmer and slightly darker than our house. The rooms were all painted earthy tones—browns and yellows and greens—and there were plenty of curtains and blinds to control the light. But the main thing I always noticed about the Patrick's house was the smell—a slightly sour mix of dog and carpet and Pinesol. I assume my house had a smell, too, but you can't smell your own house.

Jack's mother was very involved in the local church—I think she saw herself as some sort of missionary. They often took in foster children, and the house was usually filled with kids of different ages and races. I was keeping a lookout for them, but the house was pretty quiet.

Mr. Patrick was in the living room, watching TV. He was sitting in the reclining easy chair he had ordered out of a catalog—with massaging fingers and speakers built into the headrest. He had a blanket over his legs.

It took him a moment to realize that it was me—his eyesight was pretty bad—but when he did, he raised his hand in greeting. He had been a dentist, but a few years back he lopped off a finger while chopping wood in the backyard. He retired early.

"It's the honor student," he said.

"That's me." I sat on the couch, with the dogs still sniffing at my legs.

"Been studying much?"

"Here and there."

He pulled a handkerchief out of his pocket and blew his nose. "I saw something on TV about Berkeley the other day. Bunch of kids demonstrating about, what was it? Something to do with fruit?"

"Fruit bats?"

"No, no. Grapes. I think it was grapes."

"Grape nuts?"

"Very funny. No. There was some kid with a bullhorn. Looked kind of like you. Had a nasty sunburn. Were you involved in that?"

"Don't think so."

"Well, I'm relieved. I feel better now." He looked back at the TV—a thirty-inch console built into a wood cabinet. He was watching a cooking show. Some lady was stirring a bunch of brown stuff in a bowl.

"That looks good, doesn't it?"

I didn't know what it was supposed to be, but I nodded anyway.

He turned back to me when a commercial came on. "So you back for the summer?"

"Yeah. I'm gonna help my dad with the house."

"That's good," he said. "That's good."

I watched TV with him for a while—the cooking show giving way to a talk show—before noticing that Mr. Patrick had dropped off to sleep. I stood up and walked back toward Jack's room. I knew that Jack wouldn't be around— he would be on one of his training rides before he went to work at the bike shop.

Jack's room was a mess of bikes—three were piled together next to the wall. There were several extra sets of wheels, sew-up tires in various states of repair. He had a new bike in his work stand—a bright red Colnago half-built up with shiny Campagnolo components. The remaining components were still in their blue boxes on the bed. Jack had told me excitedly about the Colnago over the phone a few weeks before. To Jack, each new bike represented a new era. This was the bike he was going to ride out of here—he was planning to take it to Belgium next spring, where he was going to make a go of racing in Europe.

I walked down the hall to Mike's room. I half expected their mother to have turned the room over to one of the foster kids—or at least, I expected the door to be closed. But the door was open.

The room looked about the same—the sun-faded beer posters, the threadbare orange bedspread, and the blue-green shag carpet. But it was different. There wasn't the usual pile of dirty clothes. The bed was made and the garbage can in the corner was empty. Mike's record collection was intact, but I saw that the stereo wasn't plugged-in—the cords were carefully coiled up behind the amplifier. And the top of his desk had been cleared off—the old clutter replaced by a white doily.

Mike was Jack's older brother. He was three years older than us. Growing up, Mike had two friends—Kevin and Steve. I remember the three of them in junior high. They seemed so tough, hanging out in Mike's room, listening to AC/DC, looking at *Hustler*. But after high school Kevin went off to college and Steve joined the Air Force—he got stationed in Germany and was married by age twenty. So Mike started hanging out with us. We'd drive around in his old Barracuda—stalling out at stop lights.

Mike started working at an auto glass installation place. It was nice over there—an old building with high ceilings and big windows. Sometimes Jack and I would go there after school to help him move the cars around.

But then, during Jack and my senior year in high school, Mike quit the glass installation place and started working as the night manager at a newly opened restaurant—part of a big chain. He was working a lot of overtime and used the money to make a down payment on a new Ford Ranger pickup, which he would wash and vacuum on weekends. The Barracuda stayed parked out on the street.

So he was always asleep during the day, and working at night. Jack and I would go to the restaurant to visit him. We'd order ice water, shoot spitballs through the straws, make a mess with the salt and sugar. Mike—wearing a stupid bow tie and vest—would be formal and distant. After a while, Jack and I stopped going.

Then one day there was this new foster kid—I think her name was Lisa. I remember the tight jeans, the Sex Pistols t-shirt (I remember her saying she had met Sid Vicious and Mike teasing her about it). She had long blond hair that was kind of thin, this faint smile. I don't know how old she was. Maybe fourteen? She fought a lot with Mrs. Patrick, she stole and broke shit. So no one believed her at first.

But then everyone was all quiet and Lisa was gone—off to another foster home, I guess. I don't know what happened exactly—if Mike raped her or what—but the whole family just kind of drew back. Drew back and pretended that it hadn't happened. But it was there. It just sat there.

At first I, too, had denied what had happened with him and that girl. It all seemed kind of vague and I wasn't sure how I was supposed to feel about it, exactly. It was like in a movie when a character does something off camera. You hear about it, but you don't necessarily believe it because you didn't see it for yourself. But still, it changes something.

This all happened a few months before I went to Berkeley. Then, some time before Christmas, Mike just disappeared. His truck showed up in Los Angeles a few weeks later on a used car lot. But as far as I knew, no one had heard anything. The guy was AWOL.

I checked under the bed. The stack of porno mags was gone. The bookshelf was filled with trophies, framed photos, and model cars. There was only one book: The Guinness Book of World Records.

I took it off the shelf and started thumbing through it. There were the fat twins riding motorcycles—with the plaid pants and cowboy hats. Then there was the guy who was so huge they had to bury him in a coffin the size of a piano case. 1,069 pounds. Why did they put all the fat people up front? I flipped to the cool color photo section in the middle and saw the guy with the fingernails. They were each about three feet long and they were twisted and had these strange stripes. I had nightmares about that guy when I was a kid.

I was putting the book back on the shelf when a young Asian girl wearing a red leotard walked into the room. I assumed she was a new foster kid.

"Hi," I said.

I don't know why but I always felt really jumpy around these foster kids. I felt like they could see right through me—like they had special powers or something.

"Who are you?" she said.

"A friend of Mike's." I had meant to say a friend of Jack's.

She was quiet for a second. Then she said, "Mike's gone."

I glanced down at her pink high tops. Then I looked back at her and said, "I know."

She stood there for several seconds, then turned and walked out of the room.

Mr. Patrick was still asleep when I walked back into the living room. One of the dogs lifted its head and looked at me.

I saw then that Mrs. Patrick was in the kitchen, putting away groceries. I snuck out the back, closing the screen door quietly behind me.

Six

As I crossed back to the house, I saw Gordie pulling the last of his stuff out of the truck. He had a major case of bed head.

"There you are," Gordie said.

"Here I am."

He looked around. "So where are the mountains?"

I shrugged. "What you see is what you get."

"Kind of seems like false advertising."

I admit "Mountain View" was kind of a lame name. When you could see them, they looked more like hills, anyway. But I didn't name the place. I grabbed my last bag of clothes and we walked back inside.

When we got into the living room, Gordie dug around in one of his suitcases until he found his dental floss. He pulled it out and started flossing. Then he said, "Anything to eat?"

"Whatever you find is yours. I'm gonna take a shower."

The pipes made a horrible groaning noise and a bunch of rust and iron flakes shot out onto the shower floor. But then it settled down and I had a nice long shower.

When I came back out, Gordie was standing at the kitchen sink, inspecting the glasses.

"Are these clean?"

"If they look clean, they're clean."

"They don't look clean."

I shrugged and sat down. I rubbed my eyes. Slowly, it was starting to sink in: I was home.

Gordie washed out a glass and filled it with tap water. He took a drink and looked out the window.

"Colin?"

"Yeah."

"There's a guy passed out in your backyard."

"What?"

"Look."

I got up and looked. There was my dad, flat on his back in the weeds.

We walked outside.

"Dad?"

"Colin?"

My dad didn't move. He looked kind of peaceful there. He was wearing a shiny designer sweat suit that Gwen must have bought for him. It made him look thinner—then again, Gwen had him on a diet, too.

"What happened?" I said.

"I came over to get the ladder. I must've bent over too fast and my back went out."

I glanced over at the shiny aluminum ladder lying nearby. For the last few months my father had been transferring his things over to the new condo—but very slowly. As far as I knew, he was still planning to sell the house, but I wouldn't believe it until I saw it—my dad didn't part with things that easily.

"You okay?"

"I don't know. I think so." He wedged his hand under the small of his back and started feeling around. "But you should call Gwen. She has my pills." Then he said, "Who's your friend?"

"Oh, this is Gordie. He's gonna be staying here for a while."

"Hi Mr. Smith," Gordie said. He leaned over and shook my dad's hand.

"Nice to meet you, Gordie."

"Thank god you found him," Gwen said.

She had sped over in her old Volvo, arriving just minutes after we called. She was wearing a baggy, paint-stained sweatshirt and shorts. I had to admit she was kind of attractive—kneeling over him, so concerned, with her chubby tanned legs and cute face—but that freaked me out.

She had helped him into a fetal position and started feeding him anti-inflammatories and muscle relaxants, which he swallowed with water—half of which ran down his chin and dripped onto the dirt.

It wasn't long before Gwen had my dad up and hobbling out to her car.

I said, "You sure you don't want to stay here for a while?"

"No," Gwen said. "We have hot water bottles and bath oils at home. And the bed here is awful."

In many ways, Gwen was good for my dad. She needed more attention than my mother, and she was more dramatic, but she wasn't as judgmental. My mother was smarter, more serious. She thought my father was weak, and she had no problem saying it to his face.

Gwen had pulled the Volvo up close and pushed the front passenger seat back—all standard procedure.

My father's old Porsche 911 was parked nearby—its front bumper askew, its green paint badly oxidized. I wondered how he had planned to get the ladder in the car. But then again, he had crammed all sorts of stuff into that car over the years. He used to lash things onto the roof all the time—I'd be leaning out, holding onto a Christmas tree or some aluminum gutters my father had purchased as we went down the freeway.

My father plopped himself into the Volvo's front passenger seat. He leaned back while Gwen tried to shove his legs in.

"You ready to start on the house?" my father said.

"Sure."

"Don't worry about the yard. I'm gonna send a crew over for that."

"So, what? Paint?"

"That wouldn't hurt. But I'm going to order a dumpster. You can start going through stuff and throwing things out."

"You in?" Gwen said.

"I'm in."

Gwen closed the door on my father. She went around the other side and started the car.

"I'll come back later for the Porsche."

"Okay," I said. "Feel better."

"Will do."

With that, Gwen pulled away. Gordie and I watched them drive away.

"Your dad seems pretty cool," Gordie said.

After a while, Gordie took off to check in for his new job at the Stanford lab, leaving me alone in the house. I watched TV for a while, but then I got hungry. Two years before, I secretly made a spare set of keys for the Porsche. They were still on my keychain.

The old air-cooled engine started right up with a little burp of blue smoke. I revved it up a bit. My father wasn't too hot on me driving it. Soon after I got my license, I had tried starting it by pumping the gas like it was a carbureted V-8—killing the ancient German fuel-injection and costing my dad a pretty penny.

I drove down to the Safeway and stocked up—bread and cereal, spaghetti sauce and frozen burritos. Then I drove back home and ate.

I was watching TV again when Jack dropped by. He had just come back from work and rode right into the house on his bike—he could do that, go up steps and open doors without dismounting.

"'Sup?"

We shook hands. He swung his bag off his shoulders and leaned against the kitchen counter.

Jack was medium height but strong, muscular—he looked like a natural athlete. Coaches in high school were always trying to get him to come out for their various squads. But Jack liked to ride his bike—he liked being alone.

He had a grease smear next to his ear and his nose was sunburned. And he still had the same GI Joe haircut his mom had been giving him for years.

"How was work?" I said.

"Same old shit. You back?"

"I'm back."

"Cool." He looked around. "You sleeping in the living room now or what?"

"No, that's my roommate. He's gonna live here this summer."

"Gordie?"

"Yup."

Jack laughed and shook his head. He thought Gordie was a joke.

"I dropped by your house," I said. "Met your new sister."

Jack nodded. "Sara. She's fucking nuts."

Silence. We had been best friends for years, but now there was a bit of distance when we saw each other. And it wasn't just because of the whole thing with Mike.

Then he said, "So I gotta go for a ride, but we're gonna hang out tonight?"

"Hell yes."

"Cool."

Jack got back on his bike. "I'll come by later." He rode out the door. I heard him brush against the side of the gate as he rode out.

Gordie came home all excited. The Great Man hadn't been at the lab, but he'd been given a complete tour of the place. We made spaghetti and he told me all about it—how this intern or whatever had treated him like an "equal," how exciting the project was that they were working on, how this is what he'd been waiting for, etc. I wasn't really listening.

I got a call from my father. He had ordered the dumpster. He was glad I was home, too—"so we could talk"—whatever that meant. I asked him about his back. "It's great," he said. "Much better."

Just as we were finishing the spaghetti, Jack came by with a twelve-pack. He had just taken a shower and his hair was still wet. He had a big bag of cookies, which he dumped on the table.

"My mom sent me over with these. She doesn't want you guys to starve."

Jack's mom was like that—like one of those moms you see on TV, only real. She made the best chocolate-chip cookies in the world.

Jack was wearing a cardigan sweater and new white tennis shoes. I asked him why he was all dressed up.

"I gotta go see this girl later on," he said.

"Oh," I said. "I get it."

Gordie was silent—maybe he was thinking about his job, but I think Jack made him nervous.

"Hey," I said. "Let's get out of here, go over to the school or something."

Jack stood up. "I'm up for it."

I turned to Gordie. "You coming?"

Gordie stood up. "Sure. I guess."

It was just starting to get dark outside and the street was quiet. Jack and I lived on the edge of a big suburban maze—a long rectangle bordered by Highway 101 and the Bay to the east and Alma, a four-lane expressway, to the west. We were only two blocks from Alma, so if you stood in the middle of our street, you'd see groups of cars shoot past at 45mph, staggered by the timed lights.

We turned away from Alma and walked deeper into the maze. When we were kids, we stuck to the sidewalks, but slowly we started to take the street for ourselves, first on our BMX bikes, then with the occasional game of catch—bouncing footballs off the hoods and windshields of neighborhood cars. In high school we started walking down the middle of the street like we owned the place—when cars approached, we'd take our time moving to the side.

Our street curved around and cul-de-sacs appeared to the right and left. In all those years, I'd never learned any of the streets by name. Of course, I knew my own street name: Cortez, named after the Spanish explorer who slaughtered the Aztecs (I did a report on him in fourth grade). But otherwise, I knew the streets by the houses and the cars that were parked out front.

The elementary school was just three blocks away. We passed through some bollards, walked across the school's basketball courts and went to sit where we always did—on top of the bleachers overlooking the soccer field. This also gave us a clear view of the parking lot—in case the cops decided to swing through. The grass had just been cut and they'd gone over the whole field with an aerator, so it was covered with small holes and clumps of dirt—sure to promote dirt clod fights the next day at school. The school—a long, flat building with large plate glass windows—sat directly behind us.

Jack and I had been coming here to hang out ever since we were kids. It was the only place nearby with any open space, the only place you didn't feel watched by neighbors or parents. But now, with Gordie around, I felt self-conscious. The whole thing suddenly seemed juvenile. We were quiet as we started working through the beer.

As I pulled out my second beer, I said, "So what's the latest on Mike?"

Jack shrugged. "We got a message on the answering machine a few weeks ago. The fucker called when my parents were at church—I'm sure on purpose. Left this cryptic message. So I come back from a ride and my parents are playing that tape back over and over, like they're listening for clues or something."

I said, "Damn."

Jack shook his head. "So he's going on about how he's doing a lot of thinking, a lot of deep fucking thinking, and he's realizing some things, blah, blah, blah—he's obviously baked. Anyway, my mom started crying, and my dad got all quiet and shit. It was fucking weird."

Jack tossed a rock into the darkness. It hit a tetherball pole and made a ringing sound.

"So still no idea where he is or when he's coming back?"

"Nope." Jack finished off his beer, then burped. "Fuck if I care, either."

Then Gordie said, "Who's Mike?"

Jack stared at him for a second. "My brother."

"Oh," Gordie said.

I crushed a can and pulled out another beer from the box. A few years before we would have been smoking pot.

Mike used to get it for us, starting when we were about twelve. He liked to get us high—liked to see us get all goofy and get the munchies. He thought it was hilarious.

Sometimes, though, I'd get really paranoid—I'd sink way into myself and not talk. And Jack said he could feel it riding, too—said it made his lungs burn. But mostly, we both were turned off by the fact that Mike was so into it. That's all he ever wanted to do—get stoned and hang out. So we pretty much stopped.

By then we were a bit older. We had fake IDs and it was easy to get beer on our own. Beer is mellow. It takes a while to get drunk and it doesn't make you feel like a paranoid moron.

Jack was staring down at his new shoes. He wiped off some of the grass clippings from the field.

I said, "So who's the chiquita?"

"No one you know."

"Oh," I said. "Okay."

Jack smiled. "She's a teacher."

I laughed. "Nice."

Jack stood up and climbed down off the bleachers. "Come on." He started walking toward the school building. I grabbed what was left of the twelve-pack and followed.

"Where are you guys going?" Gordie said.

Jack climbed up a chain link fence and then pulled himself onto the flat overhang of the school's roof. I tossed up the beer and followed.

Gordie was just watching us. "Hey! What are you guys doing?"

Jack laughed. We walked across the gravel roof to the big plastic skylight and pulled it open. Jack dropped in. I followed.

We were in the library. As my eyes adjusted to the dark, I saw those same stupid posters that had been there forever—like the one that has the kitten dangling from a tree branch with the caption "Hang in there!"

In the middle of the room there was a big jar of jellybeans. Next to it there was a notebook with careful notations for all the kids who had paid five cents to guess how many jellybeans.

Jack unscrewed the jar, took some jellybeans and popped them in his mouth.

I shook my head. "Playing God." I took a few jellybeans myself. They were stale.

We headed down the hallway.

"We're adults now, you know," I said, jokingly. "This is like a felony or something."

"Fuck that," Jack said.

I followed Jack into one of the classrooms. I sat in one of the little kiddie seats, with my knees smashed up against the underside of the desk.

Outside, Gordie cupped his hands on the glass and looked in. "What are you guys doing?"

Jack was going through the teacher's desk.

"Yeah, what are you doing?" I said.

Jack took out a pen and started writing something.

"Oh shit," I said. "This is her room?"

Jack smiled. "Yup." He folded up his note and tucked it under the pencil sharpener.

I laughed and shook my head. Jack and I had been in this very classroom in third grade, pledging allegiance to the flag.

"How'd you guys meet?"

"She came into the shop," Jack said. "I fixed her bike."

"Assholes!" Gordie yelled.

Jack shook his head. "I really don't like that guy."

I went to the window to look for him but didn't see him. Then I saw the cops.

"Shit," I said. "Do they have some kind of alarm?"

"I hope not."

We went and sat in the hallway. It was hard not to laugh.

After five minutes we crawled back to the windows to take a look. They were gone.

We walked back to the house. Lights illuminated front porches, TVs flickered in windows.

"So what happened to the Barracuda?"

"Mike was trying to sell it before he took off, but then it kicked its timing chain and he was like, fuck it. After he left, my dad had it towed to Larry's. It's just sitting there."

Larry was the local mechanic—the one the Patricks always used. I said, "So Larry owns it now?"

"I think my dad has the pink slip."

"Yeah? Think he'd sell it to me?"

Jack laughed. "Man, I bet he'd give it to you."

We were standing in the middle of the street between our houses. The whole neighborhood was dark and quiet.

"Have a good time with the teacher."

Jack smiled. "I will."

Jack walked over to his motorcycle—an old Yamaha 750. He got on, started it and released the kick stand.

"See ya," he said.

With that, he accelerated away. His brake lights flashed as he turned the corner and then he was gone.

Seven

The dumpster arrived a few days later. First I heard the big diesel engine, followed by the sound of the hydraulics. Then there was a loud crash. I walked out front.

The dumpster was a big smashed-up rusted thing with a little ladder up the side. It was sitting at an angle—propped up part-way on the curb. The driver didn't seem to care.

"There you go," he said, and drove off, the back half of his vehicle reduced to a skeleton.

I had told my dad that we might make some money if we had a garage sale, but he thought that was humiliating—selling off all your old stuff. So I had been instructed to pitch out all the junk and call Goodwill to haul off the rest.

Most of it was junk. I put on work gloves and threw out plywood and old rugs, broken chairs, a rusted folding table and the snow tires from our days in Colorado. I piled the old and outdated sports equipment in the corner for Goodwill.

I was lugging out an old computer monitor when Beth pulled up in her tiny Subaru. I hadn't seen her since Christmas.

She got out and gave me a hug. She was a short girl but had a pretty good-sized chest. When she stepped back, I saw that she had a new hairstyle—short, with bangs—but otherwise she looked the same, with her big eyes and small nose. She looked like a doll.

"Hey there."

"How are you?" I said.

She just smiled at me. "What are you doing?"

"Throwing shit out."

She climbed up the ladder on the side of the dumpster, kind of sticking her ass out. "Lots of good stuff in there."

"Hey, take whatever you want."

She laughed and jumped down. "Time for a break?"

"Sure."

"Come on," she said. "I'll buy you lunch."

I had known Beth since we were little kids, and I'd had a crush on her from the start.

Beth was small now, but she was one of the biggest girls in sixth grade. In kickball she could nail the ball over the fence, and she was always one of the first picks on the playground at recess. One time, she beat the crap out of some kid when he made fun of her breasts—she got him up against the fence and kicked him repeatedly until one of the teachers pulled her off.

I think that whole experience got her looking down on kids her own age. From high school on, she had older boyfriends, and until recently, she had been seeing this guy named Dan who was in his late twenties—kind of an asshole. I think the older boyfriend thing was also a big fuck you to her father, who she hated, and who had since moved out of the house. Once, when she was twelve, in the middle of an argument with her father, she opened the car door and got out—at forty miles an hour. She rolled a couple of times and was okay except for her arm, which got pretty mangled. You could still see the scar from the surgery—a bright red lump that ran from her elbow to her wrist.

She went away to college—to Whitman in Walla Walla Washington—and when she came back for Christmas, she broke it off with Dan (from what she told me there was quite a scene—complete with vandalism and threats of violence). I guess she had a new boyfriend in Walla Walla, but I didn't know that for sure.

So from the start—or since she'd started going out with Dan, anyway—I had always felt that Beth was out of my reach. I supposed I sort of liked that. It took the tension out of our friendship. Alright, so maybe that's not quite true.

Beth's Subaru was a complete piece of shit, with torn up seats and a rear window made out of a plastic sheet held in place with duct tape. And the latch on the glove compartment door was broken so that it was always open—it bounced against your knees.

"When are you going to fix this?"

"Don't start on my car, Colin. I'll let you out right here."

"Yeah yeah."

She threw on the brakes to show me she meant it, but she couldn't keep a straight face.

We pulled into our local strip mall—basically a parking lot surrounded by an ice cream store, a record store, an auto supply store and a pathetic deli, which, until recently, had been a hangout for the heavy metal crowd. I guess they'd found a new spot.

Inside, the deli was hot and smelled like bleach. A pimply-looking kid was wiping down the counter. I thought that he might have been on our high school wrestling team—one of those kids who jogged around in full sweats on hot days and got herpes from the mats.

Beth turned to me. "What'll it be?"

"Actually, I had a late breakfast. But I'll have a Coke."

She looked disappointed. She turned to the kid and said, "One Coke, one Diet Coke." Then she stuck her tongue out at me.

We took the Cokes back outside, where there were two plastic tables with matching plastic chairs. There were holes in the middle of the tables for umbrellas, but no umbrellas. Beth first picked the table with a big pigeon shit on it, so then we had to move to the other table, which was shit free.

"Summer is here!" she said, and stretched out her arms. You could see that scar of hers, glowing.

"It's here alright."

"Aren't you glad?"

I leaned back in my chair, but the plastic legs started to buckle. I sat forward. "I guess."

"You guess? What do you mean, you guess?"

You could never give a simple answer to Beth. She always had to cross-examine you. I just shrugged.

Then Beth said, "So my mom is taking parachute lessons."

"You mean skydiving?"

"Whatever. She's learning the whole foot-knee-hip thing. They're drilling it into her."

I tried to picture it. Beth's mom was a short and fairly mild-mannered lady—though once she had held Beth's father at bay with a meat cleaver.

Beth shook her head. "She'll chicken out."

"You think?"

"Jumping? From an airplane? She'll freak."

"This some kind of mid-life crisis thing?"

"Something like that. I think she's mostly just trying to meet people." Then Beth said, "What's that guy doing?"

At first I didn't see what she was talking about. Then I saw a homeless man lying near the potted plants. The strip mall people had put the plants in two years earlier in an attempt to spiff up the place. The pink flowers died almost immediately—after suffering continual abuse from the heavy-metal crowd—and had been replaced by low-maintenance cacti. The cacti weren't giving the homeless guy much shade.

"Maybe he's resting," I said. "Taking a nap."

"Doesn't look like he's resting."

Beth got up and walked over to take a closer look. Then she walked back to our table and sat down.

"He's still breathing."

"That's good."

The deli kid walked outside and lit a cigarette. Beth pointed and said, "You seen that guy before?"

The kid shrugged.

"Maybe you should call an ambulance."

Just then the homeless guy sat up. His face was red and puffy from being pressed into the cement. He looked at the kid. "Could you spare a smoke?"

The kid walked over and gave him a cigarette. He lit it for him, then walked back past us, smirking.

Beth said, "Cigarettes cause cancer, you know."

"So does Diet Coke," the kid said. He disappeared back inside the deli.

"You try to be nice," Beth said. "See what you get?"

The truth was Beth had smoked all through high school and then had made a big deal out of quitting. Now she was self-righteous as hell.

The man lay down again but continued smoking. Every now and then a puff of smoke would appear and drift across the parking lot.

I noticed that Beth was slightly sunburned, especially on the backs of her legs.

"You got some sun."

Beth looked pleased. "Last week. The sun came out for the first time in six months. I mostly sunbathed instead of studying." Then she said, "You look pale."

"I always look pale."

Beth laughed. "That's true." Then she said, "So, have anything exciting planned?"

"Not really."

She just shook her head. "Colin!"

"I got my roommate staying with me."

"From Berkeley? I thought you hated him."

"He's not so bad."

"The guy with red hair, right?"

I nodded. "That's him."

"I definitely remember you saying you disliked him."

"I probably did," I said. "But he's okay."

The homeless guy sat up, took one last drag and stabbed out the butt on the concrete. Then he stood up and limped away. We watched as he disappeared around the corner of the auto supply store.

"Lone Samurai," Beth said.

I said, "You working this summer?"

"Yeah, at the gift shop."

"Shoppe."

"Shoppe," she said, and laughed. "I hate that place."

Beth had worked at the "Gift Shoppe" since the beginning of high school. She was the only employee who was under eighty-five. They sold all sorts of weird soap and perfume. Potpourri.

Beth yawned. "So who else is around?"

"No one. I don't know."

Beth didn't really have many friends. She had isolated herself with Dan for three years. And since going to Berkeley, I hadn't kept in touch with anyone other than Jack.

Beth shook her head. "Last summer was fun, but this summer it's like, why am I here?"

"Why are you here?" I said.

"I don't know. Why are you here?"

I shrugged.

"You're just lazy," she said. "We both are."

We just sat there for a while. An airplane made its way slowly across the sky. I watched as it disappeared over the top of the auto supply store.

"So you're going to be around?" I said.

"For a while, anyway. I might go to Tahoe later with my mom. You?"

"I guess I'll be around."

"I guess I'll be around," she said, mocking me. "You're so tough, Colin. Such a tough guy."

"You got that right."

For a while we sipped our Cokes and watched cars circle around the parking lot. Later, she dropped me off at the house. She gave me another one of those hugs and made me promise to call her. Then she drove off.

Eight

It took about a week for the excitement to wear off. Then Gordie started complaining about his job. Actually, it sounded pretty bad—mostly, he was decapitating lab rats. I guess there was a big demand for fresh rat brains.

The whole thing was pretty gruesome. Gordie would get them groggy with CO_2, then stick their heads into a miniature guillotine. After crunching down on the handle, he'd hold the decapitated body over a funnel to collect the blood. The med students referred to this process as "harvesting," and they all acted like the rats were dying noble deaths.

Anyway, it wasn't like Gordie didn't have the heart for it or anything. He just felt that his talents were being wasted. To make matters worse, the Great Man was on leave. Gordie didn't even get to hobnob.

And so at the house he was acting kind of mopey. At school, he had always been busy—he'd stay at the library until late, and when he was in the room, he was usually studying. But now, after he got home, he'd just watch TV. He'd take his shoes off and put his feet up on my dad's coffee table.

You'd think with all the free time he would've pitched in with the house. But it obviously hadn't even occurred to him. And for a guy who was so anal about his own stuff—he had already arranged his things neatly along the windowsill and on the coffee table—he didn't seem to care much about the kitchen and the bathroom. He'd leave dirty dishes in the sink and wet towels in a heap next to the toilet. I did that kind of stuff, too, but it's different when someone else does it in your place.

One night, Gordie's parents called. I knew it was them the second I answered the phone. Whenever they called, there would be a big silence on the other end, like you get when telemarketers call, and then his mom (it was always his mom, though I knew his dad was lurking on the other end) would be all formal, like she hadn't talked to me a million times before.

Gordie picked up the phone in the kitchen and pulled it into the living room, stretching the cord around the corner.

His parents seemed like a pain in the ass to me. During the year, Gordie barely talked about them, but I always got the feeling that they embarrassed him. They came to visit once. Gordie's dad was kind of like a bald version of Gordie, with a pot belly. His mom was a huge lady, and she was always out of breath. They both seemed a bit freaked out by California, and mostly complained about all the homeless people and the bad service they were getting in their hotel. Gordie had the brilliant idea to take them to this Ethiopian place—it was almost like he was trying to antagonize them. I was stupid enough to tag along.

His mom seemed pretty upset that she had to eat with her hands, but his dad was really into it—ripping his chicken apart, licking the grease off his fingers. I remember his fingernails—how they were chewed down to the quick. He was talking with his mouth open, telling me about the great deal he had gotten on their rental car. I looked at him and then I looked at Gordie, who was quietly stewing, and suddenly I understood what he was up against.

Gordie always tried to keep his phone conversations to a minimum—that was one thing we had in common, anyway. And so a few minutes later, Gordie hung up. When he walked back into the kitchen, I said, "How are mom and dad?"

"The same." Then he said, "I'm hungry."

At Berkeley we had eaten together maybe twice. But now we ate together every night.

Gordie didn't cook and I knew maybe three recipes. So mostly we went to this Mexican place near my house. We'd drive over in Gordie's truck—all of about three blocks.

I'd been going there forever—or ever since my mom moved out. To be honest, the food wasn't that great. I'd had much better Mexican food in Berkeley. But it was the experience that counted—you had to consider the whole package.

First off there was the paint job—the place was painted Pepto Bismol pink, and kind of haphazardly. There were drops of pink paint on the sidewalk and drainpipes and even on a tree that was a good ten feet from the building.

Then there were the fiberglass picnic tables that were chained together so they couldn't be stolen, and the hand-lettered menu with the prices scratched out and written over several times.

I liked the tin foil they used—I liked how it had paper on the back like the tin foil you got with hot dogs at the ballpark, and how the paper would get stained by the hot sauce, which was pretty much the best thing about the place. And then there were the Cokes—they were always flat and had too much syrup, like they hadn't been mixed right. But you looked forward to that kind of stuff, you expected it.

There was a short line at the window. People would drive up and park in the middle of the street, on the sidewalk, wherever.

The two guys directly ahead of us—both in shorts and t-shirts—were deep into a conversation about computers. The lingo seemed to change every few weeks, but it was basically the same boring conversation I'd heard a million times. One guy was getting so excited that his leg was twitching—tapping his flip-flop nervously in the dirt.

Gordie was staring at his feet, lost in thought. Maybe he was thinking about his parents, or maybe he was thinking about food—it was hard to tell. He had started wearing a Stanford baseball cap. The dark red of the hat made his hair look orange, like Bozo the Clown.

I looked around the people ahead of us to see who was working at the counter. It was a family-run business, and I had gone to school with most of the kids. Since I had gotten back, it had mostly been John—a short, stocky kid who had spent a lot of time in the school weight room. But this time it was Maria. I hadn't seen her since the previous summer.

During high school, we ended up as lab partners in chemistry. She was really smart—way smarter than me—and did most of the work for both of us. She had skin problems, and still did to a degree, but she was kind of cute. I always felt a bit odd around her—I always had the feeling she had a crush on me, and I still felt weird about letting her do all of our lab assignments. Anyway, I think she'd gotten into Berkeley but had decided to go to Foothill—the local community college—for the first few years to save money.

Finally, the middle-aged couple in front finished their order and the computer guys stepped up to the window. But of course they'd been too deep into their conversation to look at the menu or think about what they wanted.

I already knew what I was getting—two tacos with extra hot sauce and a Coke. It came to $3.87 and I was counting my change. My father always threw his change in this spittoon-type thing in his bedroom. I used to raid it all the time when I was a kid. He had built up quite a surplus while I was at Berkeley. So now I was paying for everything with dimes and nickels and pennies.

After a few minutes of confusion and indecision, the two guys finished their order. Then, just when Maria ripped off their ticket, one guy changed his drink order from a small to a medium.

Maria smiled when she saw me. "Hi Colin."

"Hi Maria," I said. She definitely looked better. I don't know what it was—maybe her hair or something. I noticed that she was wearing a necklace with a small diamond on it.

"How was Berkeley?" she said.

"Pretty good. How was Foothill?" As soon as I said it, I felt like a snob. Then I felt like a snob for feeling like a snob.

She shrugged. "Okay."

"This is Gordie. We were roommates this year."

"Hi Gordie," she said.

"Hi," Gordie said. He barely even looked at her—he was too busy squinting at the menu—which pissed me off.

Then I said, "So you working here this summer?"

"Yeah, a bit. I'm also taking a few classes."

"Oh," I said. "Cool."

"What are you doing this summer?"

I shrugged. "Hanging out. Helping my dad fix up the house a bit. That sort of thing."

"Sounds fun." She smiled. "So what'll it be?" she said.

"Two steak tacos, extra hot sauce, and a small Coke."

She wrote it down, then looked at Gordie.

"Chicken burrito and a large Coke."

She smiled and ripped off the ticket. "Be just a couple of minutes."

That last part got me—that automatic "Just a couple of minutes" that she said to everyone else. I mean, she knew me, knew I'd eaten here a million times. It probably wasn't even intentional, but it felt like a little jab.

We got our food and our Cokes and sat at one of the picnic tables. After a while, Gordie said, "So did you like growing up here?"

I was thinking about Maria—wondering who gave her that necklace. I turned and looked at him. "What kind of question is that?"

"It seems kind of boring."

"Yeah? I bet Cleveland was pretty exciting."

"I miss it."

I shrugged. "So go home."

Gordie didn't say anything.

I waved my taco in his face. "I bet they have great fucking Mexican food in Cleveland."

Gordie smiled and shook his head. "No," he said. "The Mexican food there sucks."

"See," I said.

"I don't know," he said. And then he paused, like he was about to say something profound, like he was going to admit some dark truth. I thought about his conversation with his parents earlier. Maybe that was what was eating him.

But then he said, "I guess California still seems weird to me."

I turned and looked out on El Camino—the king's highway—with its six lanes of slow-moving traffic. Cars were stopped at a light, burbling exhaust. Across the street was a motel done in a castle motif, with fake turrets and goofy balconies. I guess part of you always hates the place you're from, but there's another part of you that will take offense at an outsiders' criticism, no matter how well-founded.

I looked back at Gordie. He was still working on his burrito. The guy didn't know how to eat. He had sour cream on his face and a couple of chunks of chicken had dropped onto the table. With his job, I was amazed that he could still eat meat. Then I thought about Gordie's dad in that Ethiopian place, ripping his food apart, grease running down his chin.

Gordie noticed that I was staring at him.

"What?" he said.

"Nothing."

Nine

Jack had been pestering me to go for a ride with him since the day I got back. Finally, I gave in.

I got Jack into riding. During the ten-speed craze of the 70s, my father purchased a top-of-the-line Motobecane, which he rode maybe once. Then, when I was in high school, I dragged it out of the garage, replaced the cracked tires and went for a ride. Later, Jack joined me on an old Gitane he had bought at a garage sale. It had heavy steel rims and the chain kept coming off the front chainrings. Jack's hands were black with oil by the time we got home.

For a while there, Jack and I rode a lot together. We'd go for rides after school and on weekends. Pretty soon, though, Jack started getting serious. He wanted to race.

I did a few races with him early on. There was a series held on Thursday evenings in a big corporate parking lot. Those races were like roller derbies—fast and scary as hell. I always ended up hanging off the back, doing my best to avoid the numerous crashes. Jack would be up front, initiating attacks, chasing people down. He was strong and aggressive, and often won the chaotic sprint finishes.

Jack started wanting to go for longer and longer rides. He'd drop me on climbs and then wait for me at the top. And then he'd drop me on the fast, winding descents. Jack was always pushing himself, pushing his bike. He'd go into turns twice as fast as me and would often scrape his pedals as he pedaled through the corner. I was overly cautious, riding the brakes all the way down—my hands would ache at the bottom. The thing was to relax, Jack told me. He tried to explain some concepts of bike handling to me—something called "counter steering," a motorcycle technique where you essentially push and lean through corners. But I couldn't get the hang of it. I couldn't get into the flow.

So I pretty much stopped riding. I still had the Motobecane—it was in my room, its tires flat and the chain covered with dust. It was old and French, not a slick new Italian bike like Jack's, and it had a bunch of outdated equipment—leather toe straps and center-pull brakes. It was a fucking relic.

I was pumping up the tires when Jack came out his front door on his new Colnago. I was having trouble with my rear tire—it wasn't holding any air.

Jack circled around in the driveway. "Come on, man. Let's go."

"I think I got a flat or something."

Jack pulled to a stop. "Damn, dude." He removed his helmet and hung it over the front of his bars.

I could never get my shit together fast enough for Jack. Growing up, I'd always be late to go to school and late to go places at night. If we were going somewhere, I'd forget something and we'd have to go back. If we were in a hurry, I'd stop to tie my shoes or hesitate before climbing a fence. If we dared each other to shoplift, I'd still be looking for the smallest, most concealable item and waiting for the right moment, and Jack would already be standing out in the front parking lot with fifty candy bars stuffed down his shirt. Basically, I slowed Jack down. And he'd sigh and wait.

I pulled out the tube. Sure enough, it was split at the seam.

Jack shook his head. He took his spare tube out of his seat pack and tossed it to me.

"Thanks," I said.

And then we were rolling.

It was a nice day, sunny but not too hot. I was out there with my hairy legs and t-shirt flapping in the breeze, Jack with his tight-fitting team outfit and shaved legs.

Jack and I never really talked much on rides, and anyway, I was too out of breath to make much conversation. I started fading on the first hill—a long grind that led up and over the freeway. As we crested the top of the hill, I stopped.

"What are you doing?" Jack said. He eased into a track stand, just kind of rocking back and forth.

"I need to take a break." I took a drink from the water bottle. The water was warm and tasted like musty plastic. "Damn I'm out of shape."

Jack circled around me. "Come on," he said. He took off again—down the hill that drops into Woodside. After a moment, I started out after him.

Woodside has some of the best roads around—smooth pavement, little traffic. It's a pretty ritzy area. Big houses sit far back from the road behind long rows of redwood trees. There are swimming pools, tennis courts and stables. The traffic is made up of Mercedes and Porsches and pickups hauling horse trailers or gardening equipment.

Riding is pretty addictive—the hum of the tires, the spinning wheels, asphalt just a blur under the bike. Trees and bushes whiz by like cardboard cutouts. I understood why Jack liked it so much. You lose yourself in the speed, in the cadence. After Mike disappeared, Jack put in consecutive four-hundred-mile weeks.

I caught Jack on the flat and passed him at a full sprint, but he reeled me back in, effortlessly.

Jack sat up and took a drink from his bottle. "How you feeling?" he said, and smiled.

"Great," I said. "Perfect."

Just then, a pickup truck breezed by way too close—the rear-view mirror almost clipped my shoulder.

Jack shook his head. "Fucker." Then he sped up, started sprinting. I knew what he was gonna do. There was a stop sign ahead.

I watched as he caught the truck at the stop. He put his hand on the door and leaned in. After a second, the truck pulled away. When I caught up to Jack, he was shaking his head and laughing.

"It was a woman. Good looking, too. I gave her a bit of a shock, I think."

After that, we settled into a fairly steady rhythm. I hung back a bit, getting the benefit of a slight draft.

Once, Jack had tried to enlist his brother for some motor pacing. He got Mike to ride his motorcycle and they went out to the flats, where Jack would ride behind his brother and try to maintain the higher speeds obtainable under such a draft. But his brother had no patience for it. After a few miles, he would start messing with Jack, slowing and then increasing the speed. It made Jack furious.

Jack hadn't mentioned Mike since the first day I was back. But then, the whole family was like that—they liked the stony silence.

A few miles later, we ran into someone Jack knew, and they got into a discussion about a stage race later in the month. I'd seen this guy around before, with his old Eddy Merckx and sunburned face. When he smiled, you saw the chipped and broken teeth—the result of a crash years before. He was older and kind of a guru type to other riders. Every once in a while I'd run into these hard-core types off their bikes and it would be weird—they seemed kind of reduced.

Now that we were with this guy, the pace was increasing and I was starting to struggle. Plus, my rear derailleur had started making a horrible ticking noise. It was humiliating.

"I'm gonna turn back," I said.

"What?" Jack said. "We just started."

"You just started. I'm heading back."

"Alright," Jack said.

"Take it easy," the other guy said.

I swung around and headed back down the road. My legs ached, my chest hurt. Fuck riding.

Ten

The summer was starting to gape at me. I put my energy into the house.

Pretty soon I had cleared out the garage and had started pulling stuff out of the house. I tore the shag carpet out of my sister's old room, took down the ratty curtains from the living room and removed our broken-down screen door. I liked the feel of the work, the rhythm of it. The dumpster was filling up fast.

My dad's back was better, and he dropped by from time to time to check on my progress. He seemed pretty impressed—not just by my actually working, but by the transformation of the house.

One day while he was checking things out, he said, "Maybe I should hold onto this place. We could fix it up and actually live here again."

This was a pretty typical statement from my dad—sentimental, waffling—basically bullshit, because he didn't mean it, not if you pressed him on it. It's the kind of shit that drove my mother crazy.

I said, "What about your new place?"

My dad just shrugged. I'd been over there. It was a new duplex—one of a million look-alikes in this big new housing development.

"Everything cool with you and Gwen?"

"Everything is not cool with me and Gwen," he said. "More like the opposite of cool."

"Oh," I said. I wasn't exactly surprised, just disappointed—and not because I liked Gwen or anything. I was disappointed that my dad couldn't get his shit together for once.

My father was inspecting the paint around the front of the door, which was peeling badly. But then, it had been like that for as long as I could remember.

"The trim looks pretty bad. So why don't we start there?"

"We?" I said.

"The royal we, as in you."

"Alright."

My father turned his attention to a dead bush. He pulled off a leaf and shook his head. "The opposite of cool," he said.

My dad had a couple of girlfriends after my mom left. None of them were all that great, but I didn't really mind any of them either. What I hated was that my dad would complain about them to me. He'd say things like, "She's got a big ass." Or, "Her breath stinks." What did he want me to say?

I knew he wanted my mom back. But he'd fucked up. To be honest, they'd both fucked up—but it was probably a 60/40 or 70/30 thing, with my dad being the worst. I was glad that he never talked shit about my mom. He just acted hurt, like he was a victim or something.

After a while I gave up trying to figure out what he wanted. I don't think he knew, really, and I got sick of hearing about his problems. The dad who cried wolf.

Okay, so I'm not real forthcoming with the sympathy. I know—that's my mean streak—that's the judgmental thing that Pablo was commenting on. But more than anything, I think it's a lack of patience.

A few days later, Gwen came over. She had her kid with her—Ben. He was four years old and a real maniac, with ripped-up knees and snot coming out of his nose. When I opened the door, he shot past me and disappeared into the house.

I hadn't seen Gwen since she'd rescued my dad from his back incident. My dad said she'd been spending a lot of time in her studio—but I think he was covering for something. She seemed kind of tense, kind of tired. Her hair was all frizzy.

"Is your father here?"

"No."

"He said he'd be here."

I shrugged. "Well, he's not. I don't know where he is." And I didn't. My dad had always been somewhat mysterious in his movements. He might have been at his office—but then, he had changed offices so many times over the years that I didn't even know where it was.

Gwen frowned. I don't think she trusted me all that much. She said, "Mind if I use your phone?"

I guess I was blocking the door. I moved out of the way. "Go right ahead."

I heard a crash in the back of the house. I walked back there and found Ben in my room. He'd triggered a small avalanche off my dresser and was covered with old magazines and laundry.

"Nice going," I said.

The kid was staring at me. I felt sorry for him. He was like a runt or something. I knew Gwen was concerned about him—she was talking about putting him in a special school.

Then I thought of something. "Hey, I got a present for you."

"You do?"

"Yeah, come on."

I took him into the garage, dug around in the pile of sports equipment I had set aside for Goodwill. I stuck my old bike helmet on his head, shoved the hockey gloves on his hands. He looked ridiculous—they were way too big.

"There you go, champ."

He was freaking out, excited as hell. He turned and ran full speed into the wall. I thought he was going to start crying, but he started laughing.

His mom came around the corner. "Ben, what are you doing?"

My mother had often said the same thing to me. "Colin, what are you doing?"

I thought about my mom when I was Ben's age, falling off my bike, making a mess, pestering her to buy me toys and candy. Compared to my sister, I was a real challenge. My sister made sense—she seemed to enjoy the same things my mom had liked when she was a kid, like piano and gymnastics and stuff like that. But my mom didn't know what to do with me—I wouldn't sit still for piano lessons, and I was more interested in matches and rock fights. Once, in an attempt to channel this energy, my mom signed me up for karate lessons. But then this kid down the street got his leg broken by another kid in my class (an accident, of course, but it's like they say about young recruits who have been sent into combat—the training takes over). My mom pulled me out of the class. I was happy because I didn't like smelling other people's feet.

I was just starting high school when my mother left my father, and I certainly wasn't going to move to Arizona. Since then I had seen her maybe once or twice a year, and it had already been six months—since Christmas.

My mom called a few days later. I had only just started on the trim and there was paint all over my hands.

"Hi Colin," she said.

"Hi mom." I shoved the phone under my chin and started looking for a place to wipe my hands.

"How is everything?"

"Good."

"I bet you're happy it's summer."

"I guess."

"You finish your classes okay?"

"Yeah."

"I'm glad." Then she said, "So I hear you're helping Daddy."

"Yup," I said.

"That's good. I'm sure he could use it."

Thinly veiled criticism was one of my mother's specialties. And the farther away she was, the thinner the veil.

"Before I forget, I came across your windbreaker. Would you like me to mail it to you?"

At first I didn't know what she was talking about. Then I remembered: her new husband—the guy was actually named Dick—had given it to me when I went out there for Christmas. It had his company logo on it.

"That's okay," I said. "I don't think I'll be needing it anytime soon."

"It's not a problem," she said.

"Really," I said. "That's okay."

My mother sighed.

I said, "Could you hold on a second?"

"Sure."

I put the phone down. I just stared at it for a while. Then I picked it up.

"Look, I'm kind of in the middle of something here. I gotta go."

"Colin?"

"Yeah?"

"I love you."

"I love you too, Mom. I gotta go."

After I hung up, I looked down at my pants. I had wiped paint all over them.

Right after my mom moved to Arizona, she started her own real estate business and made a killing selling new desert homes to retirees. Dick was no slouch, either—he was some kind of corporate management-type hot shot, semi-retired. So they had a huge place—a ranch really, with tons of land. The house had a stream running through the middle of the living room and a little footbridge you could walk over. It was a joke.

So I was pretty bummed out to have to go there for Christmas vacation. But what could I do?

I actually liked Dick. He was older—in his sixties, with the golf club membership and the time-share in Aspen—and his kids were in their thirties. One of them, a Las Vegas baccarat dealer named Josh, arrived for Christmas and stayed for a few days. The two of us stayed up late every night, drinking his father's pricey scotch, talking about gambling and cars and other stupid stuff. When Josh invited me to a New Year's party in Las Vegas, I went, ignoring my mother's not-so-subtle protests. We drove out in his Monte Carlo. I can't remember much about the evening, except that I spent most of the night puking my guts out in a huge bathroom with lots of glass and stainless steel and fake marble.

I came back feeling pretty ill and spent the last few days in Arizona recuperating. My mother seemed pleased by this—by my subdued condition—and tried to engage me in these pseudo-meaningful conversations about life and fate. After I got back to Berkeley, she kept talking about what a great visit we'd had together.

Anyway, I left the windbreaker by accident. It wasn't some kind of intentional or defiant act, though I guess it seemed like one to my mother—even more so now, since I had refused to let her mail it to me. I had staked a position at random, and then refused to back down. Still,

I didn't want to call back and apologize—that would make an even bigger deal out of it.

It seemed like every conflict I had with my parents was over something small, something stupid and inconsequential. But whenever I tried to look beyond it, to what might be the larger cause or reason, I couldn't find anything—other than distance.

I knew what would happen next—my mom would talk to my sister and then my sister would call me.

My sister was busting out kids galore in Boston with her hubby, Brad. She never called until her two kids (and there was a third on the way) were in bed. So it was about 6:30 my time—9:30 her time. Gordie was watching the news and I was flipping through a pile of junk mail.

"Mom thinks you're mad at her."

"What do you mean?"

"She said you were acting funny."

"Funny weird or funny ha ha?"

"Shut up, Colin."

I'd been out to Boston once since the wedding. Saw the kids, the house and the three-car garage. Hubby tried to beat me at ping pong on their new deluxe table, but I destroyed him with my spinning serves—which he claimed were illegal.

"Seriously, you should call her back."

"I will."

"Promise?"

"No."

"Colin."

"What?"

My sister sighed. Then she said, "How's Dad?"

"The same."

"And Gwen?"

"The same."

"She lost any weight?"

"That's not nice."

My sister giggled. There was a shrill scream in the background. "Uh oh, gotta go."

"Okay."

"Just take care of yourself, okay? And take care of Dad."

"I will," I said. Then I said, "Say hi to Brad." I loved saying that.

She laughed. "I will."

I hung up.

Sometimes I missed my sister. There were times when we'd fight and not talk, but we were allies and that wouldn't change.

Gordie was flossing his teeth. The news had ended and he had started watching a nature program. I saw a herd of elephants, then a hippopotamus submerged in mud—two nostrils sticking above the surface.

I didn't feel like being in the house anymore. I stepped outside.

I was greeted by the sickly-sweet smell of rotting persimmons—the old widow next door had a big tree of them and they always made a huge mess this time of year.

I walked around the side of the house—stepping around the gas meter, ducking under the old clothesline that I couldn't remember anyone ever using. And then I was looking at the rabbit hutch. I had been putting off taking that thing apart for days.

When I was in junior high, I came across Mr. Rabbit wandering around down the street, an Easter gift abandoned to be run over or killed by a dog. One of his ears was bent, like he'd already had a close call or two.

For a few days, he hopped around my bathroom, leaving his little pellet shits all over the place. He'd cower behind the toilet when I came in, and I'd coax him out with a piece of celery.

My dad helped me build a wood-framed hutch and cover it with chicken wire. I made the door big enough so I could climb in there and spend time with Mr. Rabbit. He was a cool little guy, and easy to take care of—a sack of alfalfa would last a long time, especially when combined with a nice assortment of yard clippings. He made a big pile of shit in the corner, which smelled strongly of ammonia.

When he died, I was in high school. I buried him in the backyard. I started several holes before I found a place where I didn't hit a big rock or a pipe or something. Jack and Mike came over and we had a funeral ceremony. Mike poured beer on the grave, which kind of pissed me off.

The hutch had gotten pretty decrepit—the wood had turned gray, the chicken wire was rusted. I climbed in there one last time. I could barely fit through the door.

Sitting in the rabbit cage started making my ass cramp up, so I crawled back out. A few minutes later, I went at the hutch with wire cutters and a saw. As I worked, the sky turned dark blue and then purple.

Eleven

I was painting the front door when Mr. Patrick came out of his house.

"Colin," he said.

"Yeah?"

"Come here, I'm not going to yell."

I put down the brush and walked over. It was hot out. The sun caught me in the eye the second I started across the street.

Mr. Patrick was wearing baggy shorts, cinched tight with a belt. His pale, skinny legs stuck out below.

"Jack said you were interested in the Plymouth."

I nodded. He motioned for me to follow him.

We walked back inside the house. Mrs. Patrick was chopping carrots in the kitchen, wearing an apron and these scuffed-up blue clogs she had worn for as long as I could remember. She smiled when she saw me.

"Hello Colin," she said.

"Hi Mrs. Patrick."

I followed Mr. Patrick into his study. He had been in the Navy, and the room was filled with model boats—destroyers and aircraft carriers in glass cases. Once, when Jack was a little kid, he took one of the boats and tried to float it in the bathtub. Mr. Patrick was pretty nice about it, but he made Jack repair the damaged decals—not an easy job for a six-year-old. Jack learned not to fuck with those boats.

Mr. Patrick sat down at his desk. He opened the desk drawer and pulled out the pink slip.

"Now, Jack told you the status of said automobile?"

"He told me that it needs a new timing chain and that Mike just kind of abandoned it."

Mr. Patrick nodded. "Larry gave me a quote of four hundred dollars for the repair. I believe three hundred and fifty of that was labor."

Larry ran the local no-name gas station/tune-up shop. My father hated him—he'd fucked up the Porsche's brakes once and then tried to lie his way out of it. But he fixed all the Patricks' cars—which were mostly Japanese, nothing too weird—and so he was the one storing the Barracuda.

I said, "I think it's pretty easy, but it takes a while."

"Well, I wouldn't say that car is worth much more than four hundred dollars, even in running condition. Would you?"

"Probably not."

"You have a dollar?"

I checked my wallet. All I had was the twenty my dad had given me the day before.

"Nope. I have a twenty."

He shook his head and waved this away. He signed the pink slip and handed it to me. "You owe me a dollar."

"Yes sir."

He reached back into the drawer and pulled out the keys. I recognized that key chain right away—the little grinning skull with eyes that glowed. Mr. Patrick looked at it for a second and then handed it to me.

"Alright then."

"Thanks," I said. I felt lame, but that's all I could think to say.

Mr. Patrick wasn't really paying much attention to me—he seemed lost in thought. I got out of there.

As I walked back through the kitchen, Mrs. Patrick said, "You coming over for dinner one of these nights?"

"Sure."

"Good." She smiled.

I closed the door behind me. I pulled out the keychain and looked at it for a second. Then I walked back toward my house.

Mike bought the Barracuda for $100. It had been sitting in some old lady's garage for ten years or something. We towed it back to the house with a rope—Jack and I in Mr. Patrick's little Datsun, the clutch slipping like hell. The Barracuda's brakes were shot, and Mike rear-ended us several times before we got it home.

Mike put a lot of work and money into that car—he did a valve job and a brake job, replaced the starter and the alternator and the radiator. But it was never quite right. There was a decent amount of rust around the quarter panels, and the front end was loose. But I loved that car.

Larry, in his infinite wisdom, had parked the Barracuda behind the shop, under a eucalyptus tree. So, in addition to the busted timing chain, in addition to the flat tires and a dead battery, there was all kinds of dirt and pollen and tree sap on the car.

Still, the car looked good. The fastback design was classic—with the big glass rear window. The car was a '64, the first year of production, and it had the 273ci engine with the cool push button automatic. Mike had replaced the old steel wheels with Cragars, which made it look pretty tough. He also replaced the stock two-barrel carburetor with a four-barrel Holly to get more punch. I was excited to get it running again.

Larry agreed to lend me a jack and a torque wrench. He had the timing chain, which he sold to me for $69.95. He seemed pretty skeptical that I could pull it off, but I had helped a guy do it once in auto shop, and I didn't remember it being all that bad.

It was mostly just unbolting shit and then bolting shit back on. I removed the radiator, the water pump, and the crank pulley. That all took an hour and a badly skinned knuckle. Putting stuff back together is always the hard part. That was another two hours. Then I had to set the timing. Larry came out and gave me a hand with that.

Then, sunburned and tired, I bought a new battery, oil and an oil filter from Larry. I aired up the tires, changed the oil and topped off the rest of the fluids. The car started with a horrible shaking and rattling. Blue smoke was everywhere.

Larry was laughing, his hands shoved into the front his overalls like the village idiot. "Take it out on the freeway. Blow all that crap out."

So that's what I did, the small-block V-8 shuddering as I accelerated onto Highway 101. But slowly, it smoothed out, the engine settling into a steady hum. That old Plymouth was the best car in the world, with that big steering wheel and all those chrome gauges. Now it was mine. I let out a maniacal laugh and floored it past an ugly new BMW.

I drove home and parked the Barracuda out front. I scrubbed the shit out of it—pouring just about every cleaning product I could find in the house onto the dull red paint.

I was hosing the car off—all those toxic chemicals swirling down the storm drain—when Mrs. Greer, the old widow, came out the front door. I watched as she stepped carefully off her front porch and made her way down the walk. She was hunched over, wearing this sweater-bathrobe thing. Before her arthritis got bad, I used to see her all the time—puttering around the yard and watering her plants. She always wore this big blue hat.

Old people are a trip. Only one of my grandparents was alive—my father's mother. She lived in a retirement home in San Diego. She watched a lot of TV with her cat, Hank. Every Christmas she sent me a check for $25.

Mrs. Greer opened her mailbox and pulled out a ton of mail—I don't think she made it outside every day. Then she noticed me.

"Colin," she said. "Is that you?"

"It's me."

She walked closer. "How are you?"

"Fine. How are you?"

"Oh, not too bad, I suppose." Then she said, "Nice car you got there."

"Why thank you."

She smiled. "Very nice." She turned and started walking back toward her house. Then she said, "Now drive safe, wear your seatbelt."

"I will," I said. I didn't want to tell her that there weren't any.

After getting the Barracuda all nice and clean, I drove it over to the bike shop. I parked behind the shop and walked through the back door.

I was greeted by Sam, the old guy who owned the shop. His son was running it now, but Sam continued to hang around to pester people—making sure his employees didn't insult customers or steal stuff.

"Colin!" He was squinting at me through his Coke bottle glasses.

"Hi Sam," I said.

Sam smiled. He liked me because I worked for cheap. He paid me under the table. "You going to build some bikes for us this summer?"

"Hey, if you got bikes to build, I'll be here."

He nodded. "Good."

Jack came out of the repair area, wiping his hands on a rag.

"Hey man," he said.

"Come check out my new ride."

We walked out back. The chrome was sparkling in the sun. Jack nodded and smiled. "Looks good."

"Doesn't it?"

Jack just smiled. I couldn't tell what he was thinking—couldn't tell if he thought this was weird or what.

I said, "How's the teacher?"

"She's good."

"Yeah? So when do I get to meet her?"

"Hey, anytime. What are you doing tonight?"

"Nothing. Hanging with Gordie."

Jack smiled. "How are the rats?"

"They're dying off fast. That boy has a lot of blood on his hands."

Jeff, the head mechanic, stuck his head out the back window. "Hey Jack, get back in here."

"One second," Jack said. He turned back to me. "We're gonna see a movie tonight. You should come out with us."

"Yeah?"

"Yeah. Leave rat boy home."

I laughed. "Alright."

I walked back out to the Barracuda, which started right up. When I put it in drive, there was a nice thunk—a sure sign it needed a new U-joint. But then, it needed a lot.

Twelve

My father was there when I got home, munching on some carrots that had been rolling around in the crisper for quite some time. He was wearing his favorite t-shirt— from a 10K race he had run a decade or more ago. He was proud of that shirt. It was starting to get pretty thin.

"Colin! Good to see you!"

"Why?" I said. Often this was the precursor to a favor he wanted to ask.

"No reason."

The reason, I guessed, was that he was having more troubles with Gwen, that he wanted some distraction. But I didn't say anything.

"I thought maybe we could order some pizza. That sound good?"

"Sounds good," I said.

Gordie showed up just as the pizza arrived. Gordie seemed to really like my father. I hadn't expected this reaction—generally, Gordie was so self-obsessed he didn't take much interest in other people. And maybe this is unfair, but whenever Gordie did show interest in someone else, I always wondered about his motives.

So while we ate, Gordie asked my dad all sorts of questions about his business. My father seemed impressed by Gordie's knowledge and flattered by the attention.

I ate my pizza quickly and put my plate in the sink. It was still early but I didn't feel like hanging around with my father and Gordie any longer.

I went and brushed my teeth and put on a sweatshirt. Then went out the front door—pausing a second to say goodbye. Gordie and my dad didn't seem to notice—they were deep into a discussion about circuits.

I crossed the street to Jack's house. Mrs. Patrick was in the kitchen, pulling clean dishes out of the dishwasher.

"Hi Mrs. Patrick."

She smiled. "Hi Colin." Then she said, "I think Jack is in the shower."

"Oh, okay." I sat down at the kitchen table. I didn't want to seem unsociable.

"What are you two doing tonight?"

"I think we're going to meet up with..." And I paused—I still didn't know the teacher's name. Also, I had no idea what Jack had told his mom. He liked to keep everything pretty vague with his parents. So I said, "I think we're gonna go to a movie."

Mrs. Patrick smiled. "That sounds like fun." She put a stack of dishes up in the cupboard.

A friend of Mike's once asked, "Does your mom smoke pot?" No one could believe she was so mellow. Sometimes, the calm silence would really unnerve me. Mrs. Patrick was facing away from me, wiping off the counter. I almost expected her head to swivel around like Linda Blair in The Exorcist. I looked down at her feet—at those blue clogs. The kitchen clock ticked softly behind me.

A minute later Sara came in. She was wearing a hooded sweatshirt and was chewing on one of the drawstrings. She sat across from me, took the drawstring out of her mouth and stared at me intently.

"Hi," I said.

She frowned, then pulled the hood over her head and cinched up the drawstring so all you could see was her nose.

Mrs. Patrick turned around. "Sara," she said. "What are you doing?"

"She's hiding," I said.

Sara shook her head. Then she pulled off the hood and stuck out her tongue.

"Don't be rude, Sara," Mrs. Patrick said gently.

Sara shrugged. She got up, walked over to the fridge, and opened the door. She hung on the door for several seconds, then closed it. She turned to see if we were paying attention. Then she opened the door and closed it, and then opened the door and closed it again.

Mrs. Patrick said, "Sara, the refrigerator isn't a toy."

Sara made her arms into airplane wings and flew out of the room.

Mrs. Patrick sighed, then went back to wiping off the counter.

At that point, Jack walked in. He nodded at me, then gave his mom a kiss on the cheek. "I'll see you later."

"Bye dear," Mrs. Patrick said. "Have fun."

Jack and I went outside and I fired up the Barracuda. It didn't seem weird until we were actually driving. Before it had been daylight. Now it was dark and it was me and Jack and no Mike.

Jack was dressed up in his country-club tennis-pro outfit again, and he was wearing some really sick-smelling cologne.

"You take a bath in that shit?"

"What?"

"Stinks." I rolled down my window.

Jack laughed. "Fuck you."

After a few blocks, Jack leaned forward and turned on the radio. The dash-mounted speakers burped to life with a bunch of static which turned into this horrible thumping sound. Jack laughed and shut it off. "I forgot."

Jack opened the glove compartment and a ton of crap fell out. When I looked over, I saw Jack holding Mike's Buck knife. Mike had owned that knife forever—he used to play with it all the time. Mostly he would just throw it at stuff, which was a really irritating habit. One time he threw it and it bounced off a tree and caught Jack in the leg. This was maybe three years before, but Jack was already bigger than Mike, and stronger. Jack jumped on Mike, held the knife in his face and made him promise to never do that again.

Jack stuffed the knife back in the glove compartment.

"What do you think Mike's doing right now?" I said.

"Who knows."

"Probably smoking some really shitty Mexican pot."

Jack said, "I'm starting to think he's dead."

"What?" I said. "Why?"

Jack shrugged.

"Maybe he's faking his death. Like Jim Morrison or something." This was supposed to be a joke—Jack and I had gone through a bit of a Doors phase in high school.

Jack smiled and looked out the window. "Maybe."

The teacher lived in a mother-in-law apartment behind someone's house. It was basically a converted garage. We walked through a little gate and cut through the backyard.

By now I was pretty damn curious to meet her. Jack had told me that she had recently dumped her fiancé, who was a hot-shot lawyer in San Francisco.

She came out wearing new-looking jeans and a pink sweatshirt. Jack always went for the wholesome type—the girl next door and all that. But she was a beauty. Long legs. Long blond hair. She seemed younger than I had imagined. I guess she was twenty-three.

"This is Jill," he said.

"Jack and Jill?"

Jack smiled. "That's right."

Jill said, "Nice to meet you."

She closed the door behind her, saying her place was too messy for me to see. Jack kidded her about it and we walked back out to the car.

I'm sure Jack had told her about Mike, but he didn't say one word about the car. I was glad.

Jill wanted to see *Die Hard* but it was sold out, so we ended up seeing *Rambo III*, which was stupid as hell. I think Stallone took on the entire Soviet army or something. I don't remember. What I do remember is being fucking jealous—Jack and Jill all cuddled up together, sharing a box of red licorice. Plus, the whole thing with the car and Mike's Buck knife had put me in a weird mood.

I got up to take a piss and then spent the rest of the movie hanging out in the lobby, playing Asteroids.

You don't see Asteroids that much anymore. I guess it's not flashy enough—there are no big explosions, no crazy colors or sound effects. It's more about finesse. There's a real calmness that comes over you as you maneuver your spaceship around the big, slow-moving boulders and whizzing rocks. Occasionally an alien spacecraft will venture across the screen and spoil the mood, but they're pretty easy to destroy, and worth the big points.

After a while, I racked up a bunch of bonus ships—stacked up in the top corner of the screen. And then I noticed that this little kid was watching—standing right next to me, mesmerized. So when the movie got out, I let him take over. He looked confused at first—confused at my just giving him the game—but then he got right in there.

Jack and Jill were almost the last ones out of the theater. Jack had never watched credits before. Maybe Jill was into that.

Jack had to go to the bathroom, so then I was just standing there with Jill. She smiled at me, then looked down at her pink sweatshirt and started picking at some lint.

I said, "You like the movie?"

"No," she said, and laughed. "It was horrible." Then she said, "So Jack said you guys are best friends."

"Pretty much," I said.

"That's great." Then she said, "My best friend lives in New York now."

I hate the way people say "New York" like you're supposed to be impressed—like just living there is a big achievement. I said, "Oh yeah? What does she do there?"

"She's a dancer."

"Well that's impressive."

Jill laughed but she looked kind of annoyed. "It is?"

"I don't know," I said. And all of a sudden, I decided I didn't like this Jill person much. Or, to put it another way, I liked her fine but I had nothing really to say to her.

Jack came out of the bathroom. I guess to him it looked like we were having a good old time because he smiled and said, "What are you guys talking about?"

I said, "New York, dance. That kind of thing."

Jill just smiled. I think she thought I was lame.

No one said much of anything in the car. I dropped them off at Jill's place and went home.

When I pulled up in front of the house it was still pretty early—just after ten o'clock. My dad's car was gone, but Beth's Subaru was parked in the driveway. The engine was still ticking.

I walked in to find Beth and Gordie sitting at the kitchen table. Beth had her hair done in all these mini pig tails.

"Hi Colin," Beth said.

"You look like Pippi Longstocking."

"Shut up."

"I guess you need more freckles."

Beth was picking at a piece of leftover crust from the pizza box. "So Gordie here was just telling me all the horrible things you said about me."

"No I wasn't," Gordie said. His face turned red.

I sat down at the table. I couldn't think of anything to say. I looked at Beth, then at Gordie. An odd combination.

Beth pushed her chair back and kicked off her Keds. "Do my feet stink?"

She pulled one of her legs toward her face and smelled her foot. She had been a gymnast and was practically a contortionist.Gordie was watching, amazed.

I guess she was satisfied that her feet didn't smell. So then she said, "Anyway, we were thinking of going swimming."

I looked at my watch. "The pool's closed."

"Good," Beth said. "We'll have the place to ourselves."

Gordie was always weird with girls. There was one girl at the beginning of the school year—this tall, bookish girl who seemed insecure and pompous at the same time. Whatever was going on between them, it didn't last long. There were some strange phone calls—with Gordie saying "no" over and over again—and then I never saw her again.

Then there was the girl who came to visit from Ohio. She was a year younger than us and got her parents to pay for a little college tour. She was kind of cute—with this funny page-boy haircut—but she was kind of runty, and really needy.

Anyway, I felt sorry for her. She slept on our floor for a week, and the whole time, Gordie was a complete asshole. He kept shoving her stuff into the corner, and he made her roll up her sleeping bag every morning. I made the mistake of being civil to her and she glommed onto me—following me to class and the library and cafeteria. The last few days were the worst—with Gordie alternately ignoring her or being openly hostile. I asked Gordie about her after she finally left, but he clammed up and refused to say a word.

The local swim club was a small place with a pool and a couple of tennis courts. A few years back, some drunk kid dove into the shallow end after hours and ended up paralyzed. There were threats of a lawsuit and the typical community concern-type bullshit. Then, a while later, someone broke in at night and vandalized the place— breaking windows, knocking the Coke machine over and throwing the deck chairs into the pool. The upshot of all this was that they'd put in a taller fence, and there was even some talk about installing an alarm. But if you didn't make too much noise and kept an eye out for cops, you could swim there at night without too much trouble.

I climbed over the fence and went around to let them in through the front gate. The pool lights were all off and the water looked black.

Beth didn't hesitate—she immediately took off all her clothes and jumped in. Gordie was pretty blown away. He turned and looked at me.

I just laughed. I couldn't help it. Gordie, of course, thought I was laughing at him—which was only partly true. He said, "Fuck you."

"What?" I said. And then I felt it—blood running down the back of my throat. I sat on the grass and lay back.

Beth was splashing around in the water. "Come on!" she yelled.

"What's wrong?" Gordie said.

"Fucking bloody nose."

"Come on!" Beth yelled, again.

Gordie turned to Beth. "He has a bloody nose."

"What?"

"A bloody nose!"

Suddenly, Beth was at my side, naked and dripping wet. "You okay?"

"Fine. I'm fine. Go swimming."

She looked at Gordie. "What's your excuse?"

Gordie looked confused. I could tell even in the dark that he was blushing. He started to undress, stopping at his tighty-whities.

Beth smiled. "Scared?"

"No," he said.

"He has a war wound," I said. When I laughed, even more blood poured down the back of my throat.

"Fuck you," Gordie said.

Beth laughed and jumped back in the water.

Gordie looked at me, then he took off his underwear and jumped in.

I heard Beth say, "That wasn't so difficult, was it?"

Above, the sky was dark, except for a few smallish clouds that glowed a bit in the moonlight.

I think this only happens at night when I'm tired or drunk or high, but I started feeling like I was weightless, like I wasn't there at all. And there was this other feeling—this vague feeling of nostalgia that always makes me feel slightly sick, like somehow I'm missing out on something, like I'm already some pathetic senior citizen looking back on the "good old days."

I sat up. But then the blood started flowing and I had to lie back again. So then I just lay there, listening to the laughing and splashing.

We walked back to the house—Gordie and Beth wet under their clothes. We stopped in front of Beth's car.

Beth said, "Well, I guess I should go home."

There was a light breeze, and Beth was shivering—her lips were blue.

"Nice meeting you, Gordie."

"Nice meeting you," Gordie said, all formal.

Beth giggled and opened the car door. The dome light came on, illuminating the black vinyl interior of the car.

Then Beth said, "We're being watched."

I turned just in time to see my yuppie neighbor peeking through the front shades. The shades fell back.

Beth laughed. "Peek-a-boo!"

"It is late," Gordie said.

"Never too late for losers." Beth started the car. "See you guys."

"Bye Pippi."

She gave me the finger and drove away.

I turned to head inside. When I got to the front door, I saw that Gordie was still standing in the street.

"You coming?" I said.
"Yeah," Gordie said, all distracted.

Thirteen

I was on the train. Pablo had called a few days before, and so now I was on my way up to San Francisco. I didn't take the Barracuda because I always got lost driving around San Francisco—I always ended up going the wrong way on one-way streets. Also, I didn't trust the Plymouth's brakes on those steep hills.

The train was slow, stopping every mile or two. After a few stops, the conductor came around and punched my ticket. I was sitting in the single seats up above the double seats, looking down on people through the stainless-steel luggage racks. The train was filled with business types reading the newspaper, many with their shoes off, their feet propped up on the opposite seat. There were also a few old men going to the racetrack—guys who hadn't had a shower in a while, taking sips from cans in brown bags and studying their racing forms. In front of me, a middle-aged woman was reading a paperback. She had her knees pulled up and her skirt tucked under her.

I turned and looked out the scratched-up windows as the landscape slid past. New car lots broke off and expanded into trash-strewn fields, with abandoned shopping carts here and there. Then a series of apartment buildings built right up against the tracks—an old guy stepping out his front door in his underwear to scowl at the train—then fields again, the sun jutting in and out behind the trees.

Then I saw the kids, hunkered down in the ditch beside the track. The brick was already airborne—it seemed to freeze for a moment just before it hit the window—then BAM! People jumped, yelled out, then a few laughed and shook their heads. I turned to catch a glimpse of those kids, so excited, jumping up and down and laughing and patting each other on the back. Jack and I had put stuff on the tracks and thrown things at the train before, but we'd never gotten up the nerve to throw anything as large as a brick.

When the brick hit, the woman ahead of me had made quite a yelp. I saw that she was shaking.

"You okay?" I said.

She looked at me and managed to nod, yes.

I smiled. "Kids."

It was a bit of a walk from the train station. Pablo lived on Potrero Hill, a neighborhood cut off from the rest of the city by freeways. I made my way up one steep block after another. Cars were parked precariously—wheels turned in, tires pinched against the curb.

The views were pretty incredible—the skyscrapers downtown in one direction, the shipyards of Hunter's Point in the other. And you could see clear across the Bay, through a thin layer of smog, to Oakland.

The street was pretty much deserted. I walked past an old lady walking a small dog with a limp. Later, I came across a guy working on his motorcycle. He was taking up the whole sidewalk, with a bunch of parts laid out on greasy rags. He was swirling something around in a dirty mason jar filled with gasoline. I stepped around him.

I found Pablo's place, a big old Victorian with its white paint peeling. Pablo's voice crackled over the intercom, and then he buzzed me in. I walked through a narrow alleyway and climbed up the back stairs—more like a big old rickety fire escape than stairs, with people's potted plants, laundry, and kitty litter boxes crowding the way.

Pablo leaned over the railing and looked down at me. "Hey you loser."

It looked like he had just woken up—he was still wearing his bathrobe. Or maybe he was going for some kind of decadent effect.

The apartment reeked of incense. We walked through a narrow hallway with worn hardwood floors and dingy walls, then pushed through long strings of beads to enter the living room.

Pablo had told me about his roommate, Lenny. He'd been busted on some kind of sodomy charge in Louisiana in the 60s but had managed to hop bail and escape to Canada. Now he was back in the States, living under a fake name and working in the financial district. Lenny was worried that people were going to find him out—worried that he could be thrown back in jail—and he made Pablo answer the phone. It was kind of pathetic that he confided so much in Pablo.

I was relieved that the roommate wasn't around. Pablo disrupted the sleep of a big old Maine Coon cat so I could have a place to sit on the ratty mustard-colored couch.

"Cool cat," I said.

"He has leukemia."

I said, "What?" and laughed. I couldn't help it.

"Yeah, he's gonna die soon. Lenny's pretty bummed out about it."

The cat sat on the floor and started licking its butt.

Pablo said, "So what's up?"

"Not much. What's up with you?"

Pablo shrugged. "The usual. Hey, want a beer or something?"

"Alright."

Pablo got a couple of beers from the kitchen, came back and handed me one.

I popped mine, took a sip. Pablo sat on the edge of the couch with his bathrobe falling open.

I shielded my eyes. "Dude, I don't want to see that."

"Oh," Pablo said. "Sorry."

A group of small black flies were circling around the middle of the room, making jerky zigzags.

Pablo shook his head, stood up. "You can't keep the windows open in here or you get these little fuckers."

He left the room, then came back with a blanket. He used it to herd the flies out the window. It took him a couple of runs, but eventually he got all of them out and then shut the window.

"Nice going," I said.

"Hey, thanks."

I took another sip of my beer. "So what are we gonna do?"

"I got some plans. In fact..." Pablo looked at his watch. "Shit. We gotta go." He got up and walked back out of the room.

"Where are we going?"

Pablo called out from the bedroom. "To the airport. Clarissa is coming into town."

Clarissa was Pablo's old girlfriend. She had gone down to Santa Barbara for school and was only getting home now. It was typical that Pablo wouldn't mention this until now.

He came back in, pulling his sweatshirt over his head.

"You done with that?" he said.

"Hold on." I quickly swallowed the rest of my beer.

The cab driver floored it onto 101, cut across four lanes of traffic and started tailgating a van in the left lane. The freeway took us past Candlestick Park, then dropped down to skirt alongside the Bay. The cab driver smelled bad. His hair was matted down under a greasy baseball cap and his vinyl jacket was stained around the shoulders.

Pablo had brought along a bottle of tequila for the cab ride, and we passed it back and forth. I had to shake my head after each sip. The stuff burned.

As we got closer to the airport, Pablo said, "Man."

When I didn't say anything, he shook his head and let out a sigh. So I gave in and said, "What?"

"I don't know."

Sometimes, Pablo bugged the shit out of me. I just stared at him. Then he said, "She's just been calling me a lot. You know what I mean? It's irritating."

"Why?"

Pablo shrugged. This was his I'm-callous-as-hell-but-still-want-your-sympathy mode. Pablo was basically a hypocrite, but if you called him on it, he'd fess up.

"Man, just shut up," I said.

Pablo laughed. "Yeah, okay."

We got to the gate just as the last people were coming off the plane.

"Shit," Pablo said. He dropped himself into one of the molded plastic chairs.

"Maybe we should check the baggage claim area."

"Yeah." He stood up. "Okay."

A red light started flashing and the conveyor belt stopped, leaving only a bag of golf clubs and a mangled cardboard box.

Pablo was pacing back and forth. "Maybe I fucked up. Maybe she's coming tomorrow." He fished around in his pocket until he came up with a crumpled piece of paper. "I should call her mom."

I followed him to the phones. Just as he started talking to the operator, a hand reached from behind us and tapped Pablo on the shoulder.

It was Clarissa, smiling.

I had met Clarissa twice before—at Christmas and Spring break. She came from a wealthy Alameda family and her father was a lawyer. She seemed kind of stupid sometimes, but I liked her, with her freckles and too much eye makeup.

She and Pablo had some kind of open relationship thing going, I wasn't sure how it worked.

We finished the tequila on the cab ride back to his apartment—this time being driven in a more sane manner by an old Indian guy. Pablo and Clarissa kept squirming around and whispering like a couple of kindergartners. I looked out the window.

When the cab dropped us off, Clarissa said, "You live here?"

"Yeah," Pablo said. "What did you expect?"

"Nothing," Clarissa said, and laughed.

I could tell they wanted to be alone for a while, so I walked out to the corner market to get some food and took my time.

The rush of tequila had worn off by the time I got back. Pablo and Clarissa looked kind of sleepy. We made some quesadillas in the microwave and drank beer. Then Clarissa brewed a big pot of coffee so we could wake up a bit.

After a while, Pablo said, "So there's this party if you guys want to go."

"Where?" I said.

"At some friend of my sister's. It's in the Mission. We can walk."

Clarissa scoffed. "We can't walk."

"Yeah we can. What? It'll be easy."

Clarissa shrugged. "Whatever you say."

We were lost in about ten minutes. To top it off, the fog had rolled in. The air was damp and cold.

"Where the fuck are we?" I said.

"I don't know," Pablo said. "Shit."

We were standing at the bottom of a hill, surrounded by houses with bars on the windows. The freeway was nearby—we could hear it, but it was behind a large wall.

Pablo bent down—he had something in his shoe.

Clarissa hugged herself and smirked. "Good thing we walked."

Pablo stood up again, pointed

"Hey, there's a bus."

An electric bus was moving slowly across the inter-section—wires crackling, shooting sparks.

We ran for it.

We sat in back, the only people on the bus. A beer can rolled back and forth under the seats.

"Are we going the right way?" Clarissa said.

Rows of faceless Victorians slid past looking like black and white photos.

"I don't recognize anything," I said.

"I'll ask," Pablo said. He walked to the front of the bus.

Clarissa looked at me and laughed. Sometimes I felt like we were compatriots or allies. She seemed to have pretty much the same take on Pablo that I did.

A moment later, Pablo walked back shaking his head.

"That guy's an asshole."

"Let's get off," Clarissa said.

Pablo grabbed the cord and yanked. It slapped limply against the window. We went right past a stop.

"Hey!" Pablo yelled.

The driver threw on the brakes and swerved toward the curb. The back door flopped open.

Pablo yelled "Fuck you!" as the bus pulled away.

"Oh gross," Clarissa said. "Someone left gum on the seat."

Pablo laughed. "You got gum on your butt?"

Clarissa twisted around. "I got gum on my butt."

"What flavor?" I said.

"Shut up," Clarissa said, laughing. Then she said, "I think it's peppermint."

"She's got gum on her butt," Pablo said.

Oddly enough, the bus had brought us in the right direction. It was just a matter of blocks.

We walked down a wide road with palm trees, Pablo and Clarissa holding hands, Clarissa humming something to herself.

We turned up what was supposedly the right street.

"See?" Pablo said. "It's all under control."

"We never doubted you, honey," Clarissa said.

"Yeah you did," Pablo said. "You doubted."

A sign was taped to the door: "Come on in!" The door was open.

We walked up a long staircase, through an empty apartment, then out the back door and down steep steps into a dark backyard. Candles flickered in glass jars, the flames throwing long shadows against the fence and surrounding houses. The yard was like a jungle, filled with sunflowers and snapdragons.

People were clustered in small groups, talking quietly, with the occasional outburst of laughter. A few girls with shaved heads turned to look at us, then went back to their conversation.

Clarissa said, "I thought you said your sister was going to be here."

"That's what she told me," Pablo said.

Behind me, two women were sitting cross-legged on the ground. They had a little plastic wind up toy—one of those chattering teeth gizmos they give kids at the dentist. They kept winding it up and letting it jump around in the dirt.

"Beer," Pablo said. "Where's the beer?"

I shrugged. Then I saw Pablo's sister Anne walking toward us with some girl I recognized but couldn't quite place.

"Look," I said.

Anne and Clarissa screamed and hugged each other. Now I knew who the girl was: Mercedes Steve's sister. She looked different in the dark. Maybe her hair was shorter or she was tanner or something. Plus she was wearing baggy overalls. I was trying to remember her name.

"Hi," Pablo said. "I'm Pablo. I think we met."

"Yes. I'm Chloe."

"How you doing, Chloe?"

"Okay." She looked at me. "And you are..?"

"Colin," I said.

"That's right," she said. "I remember."

I, of course, was quite pleased with this response. Anne and Clarissa ran off somewhere arm in arm.

Pablo was staring at Chloe's beer. "Where'd you get that?"

Chloe turned and pointed. "Over there."

Pablo walked off to get the beer.

I said, "Where's Steve?"

"Parking," Chloe said. She rolled her eyes.

I smiled. "Worried about the car?"

"You could say that."

I just nodded. Silence.

"So…" she said. She let one foot slide forward, then pulled it back. Then she looked at her sneaker and wrinkled her nose. "Dirty back here."

"Yup. Really dirty."

She wiped the dust off her shoe. "Gosh darn dirt." Then she said, "So you go to Berkeley, right?"

Here it was, the necessary drivel. I always wanted to skip past this stuff but I had never figured out how.

"So far. And you?" I couldn't figure out how old she was. She could have been seventeen or twenty-seven.

"I just finished my second year at Wellesley."

"Wesly?"

"Wellesley. You know. Small. Cold. Boring."

"Where's that? Maine or something?"

"Massachusetts."

"Oh, right."

Pablo reappeared with beers and handed me one. We all just stared at each other. Pablo took a sip of his beer and burped.

"Thank you," I said.

"Yes, that was very nice," Chloe said.

Pablo smiled. "Thanks."

No one said anything for a moment. Then Pablo said, "Does your sternum ever pop?"

I shook my head. Chloe laughed.

Clarissa walked up and draped herself over Pablo. "I'm tired."

"How can you be tired? We just got here."

"I just am."

Pablo looked at me and shrugged. "She's got gum on her butt."

Clarissa pouted her lips. "Take me home."

Anne had joined us. She punched her brother on the arm. "Take her home."

"Alright, alright." He turned to me. "What are you going to do?"

Anne said, "Stay."

I shrugged. "I guess I'll stay."

"Alright," Pablo said. "I'll leave the door unlocked."

"Cool," I said.

"Oh," Pablo said. "I guess I better give you these." He pulled four more beers out of his jacket.

Chloe laughed. "Stocking up?"

"You never know," Pablo said. "Sometimes they run out of beer early at these parties. Then you're fucked."

They left, but not before Pablo had given me this irritating leer that I'm sure Chloe caught.

Mercedes Steve showed up a few minutes later, wearing a new leather jacket that was too small for him.

"This party sucks," he said.

"I'm sorry," Anne said.

"It's all your fault," Chloe said, sternly. The two of us were working our way through Pablo's stash of beer.

Steve said, "Your friends always have weak parties."

"She's not really my friend," Anne said.

"Where is she, anyway?" Steve said.

Anne looked around, shrugged. "I don't know."

Chloe said, "So let's go somewhere else."

Chloe and I sat in back. Mercedes Steve made Anne stand on the curb and direct him out of the parking space—he was wedged in between a van and a motorcycle. It took him a few back-and-forths, and then Anne jumped in and we were out of there.

I had been fine standing up, but now that I was cooped up in a moving vehicle, I started getting the spins. Spins always felt like some cheesy effect from an old movie, except that they were often accompanied by sudden surges of nausea.

Mercedes Steve switched on the radio, then turned up the volume when this pathetic 70s-sounding rock song came on.

"What the hell is this?" I said.

"Red Rider," Mercedes Steve said. "Lunatic Fringe."

"They're singing about their fan base," Chloe said.

Anne turned around in the seat. "So where do you guys want to go?"

Chloe said, "I don't care." She looked at me. "What do you think?"

"No idea."

"Oh, come on," she said. "You must know some good places."

"Yeah, but I'm not telling."

Steve said, "I know a bar."

Then we were at the bar. I got in with my fake ID, somehow, and walked to the bathroom.

After pissing for about an hour, I went and looked at myself in the stainless-steel mirror. It's funny how you don't look drunk to yourself when you're drunk. You either look tired or suave or a mix of the two.

When I got back, Chloe was talking to some guy with a scarf—or rather, he was talking to her. She didn't seem to be listening all that closely.

The guy said, "I try to keep an open mind about those sorts of things."

Chloe turned to me with a little smirk. "How about you? Do you have an open mind?"

"My mind is narrow."

It wasn't even close to funny, but Chloe laughed anyway. The guy looked irritated and excused himself.

Anne asked me for some quarters, then went over to the jukebox and started flipping through the selections. Meanwhile, Mercedes Steve was being condescending as hell with the bartender, ordering some fancy mixed drinks. He looked at me. "What do you want?"

"Whatever."

Mercedes Steve handed me a drink. I took a sip, nearly spit it out.

"What is this?"

Mercedes Steve frowned. "A fuzzy navel."

"A what?"

Chloe said, "I'll trade you."

"What do you have?"

She laughed. "I don't know."

Then, when Chloe walked off to the bathroom, Mercedes Steve said, "She has a boyfriend, you know."

Later, I was sitting at the bar. I had switched back to beer after the weird mixed drink, but I had the feeling the damage was done—I was feeling ill.

There was an old guy sitting on the stool next to me. He had a duffel bag on the ground near his feet, and he started taking out these little Civil War toy figures. At first I wasn't really paying much attention—I was just trying to keep my shit together. But pretty soon he had a whole regiment on the bar.

So I took a closer look. The soldiers were all hand-painted with this crazy amount of detail. Some of them looked angry, some of them looked scared or indifferent. I couldn't tell you if they were Union or Confederate—I didn't pay all that much attention in American History—but it was like I was down there on the battlefield. I was looking at those soldiers and they were looking right back at me.

Then I noticed that some guy was leaning over me. When I turned, he said, "Can I play?" And then he gave me this look, this condescending smirk.

I said, "Fuck you."

"Excuse me?"

"Why don't you fuck off?" I said.

I'm not the biggest guy, but I guess there's something about the way I look that communicates that I'm not worth messing with. I'd had a few confrontations in

Berkeley with frat boys and had found that they'd usually back down quick. Pablo said I didn't look like the kind of guy who'd fight fair—and he was probably right. Anyway, the guy just shook his head and walked off.

After a while, the old guy started putting away his little soldiers. He looked at me, nodded, then handed me a soldier. Then he got up and walked out.

Just then, Chloe walked up. "Who was that?"

I shrugged. I was looking at the soldier. He had his bayonet out. There was blood on it.

I showed it to Chloe. She said, "Scary."

Next thing I remember, I was being dropped off at Pablo's place. Chloe got out and gave me a hug. She said, "Bye. Hope to see you again."

"Yeah," I said.

I waited until the Mercedes had disappeared down the long hill, then I walked over to some bushes and threw up.

After that, I felt pretty good. I felt like I could go for a run around the block or something. I took Pablo's steps two at a time, but in my enthusiasm, I tripped and almost broke my shin. After that, it was one foot in front of the other the rest of the way up.

When I walked in, a voice said, "Hello?"

"Hi," I said. Then I said, "I'm Pablo's friend."

I pushed through those beads and walked in the living room. The guy was sitting on the couch, watching a video.

"Hi. I'm Lenny," he said.

He didn't look like I had imagined him. He was small and balding, wearing cut-offs and orange basketball shoes without laces. The dying cat was sitting in his lap.

"Where were you planning to sleep?"

I shrugged. "I have no idea."

"I suppose you should sleep in here. Do you mind if I watch the rest of this movie?"

"No," I said. "Go right ahead."

I walked into the bathroom and drank water directly from the faucet.

I spent some more time in the bathroom, just looking at stuff. There wasn't much to look at—a dying fern, a few disposable razors, a tube of toothpaste. I picked up a can of shaving cream and noted that it was rusty on the bottom. Then I put it back.

I sat on the tub and then I stood up. I wanted to be asleep. I wanted to not be drunk. I wanted to be somewhere else. I thought about Chloe but then I didn't know what to think. So I just stood there for a while feeling like a trapped idiot.

The movie was a Western, with long gun battles and lots of screaming. I slumped down on the couch and let the images wash over my face.

I woke up to an explosion of static—the tape had run out and the VCR had started rewinding. The room was empty. I shut off the TV and went back to sleep.

Later, the cat started walking around me, purring. It smelled like cat food and, I thought, disease. I pushed it away.

Fourteen

I got home to find Gordie on the couch, watching Saturday morning cartoons.

Gordie said, "He's here."

"Who?"

"Your dad."

"So?"

"No, I mean he moved back in."

"What?"

"He had a big blow up with what's her name."

"Gwen."

"Yeah, Gwen."

My dad was in his bedroom, pushing boxes around. His bed was made, clean shirts were stacked on his dresser. He turned as I walked in.

"Oh, hi Colin."

"Gordie told me what happened."

"Nothing happened, exactly."

"You and Gwen split up?"

My dad sat on the bed and ran his hands through his hair. "I just need some time to think."

"Does she know about this?"

"About what?"

"About you being over here."

"Of course."

I didn't really know what to say. "So now what?"

He shrugged. "There's no hurry. No one's rushing to any conclusions."

"Okay, Dad." I started to walk out of the room.

"I thought maybe I could help you with the house. We can work on it together."

I turned back and looked at him. He looked really old all of a sudden—kind of small and sad.

"Whatever you want."

It was weird having my father around. I wasn't used to it. He woke up early and made a lot of noise, bashing around in the kitchen. And he was always complaining that he couldn't find things. I kept having to track down stuff for him, like keys or nail clippers or the saltshaker.

But the worst thing was the positive attitude and youthful energy routine—the singing in the shower, the morning calisthenics, the herbal tea instead of coffee. All this had started with Gwen, and it continued, even in her absence. She had taught him something called "the sun salute," and so in the morning I'd see him outside my window—out in the weeds—reaching up to the sky and then bending down to touch his toes. I think I preferred the pre-Gwen dad. The beat-down, depressed dad. The dad with some sense of shame.

One morning I walked into the kitchen to find him sitting at the table with a bunch of catalogs.

"What do you think about our cabinets?" he asked.

"I don't know."

"I think they're ugly," he said. Then he added, "Your mother always hated them."

I shrugged. "They're cabinets."

"Well, I was looking through some of these catalogs here. You can get some pretty decent stuff these days for cheap."

I got a bowl and a box of cereal and sat down.

"So you up for it?" he said.

"Up for what?"

"Up for a little home improvement."

"I thought you were selling the place."

"It will make it look better to potential buyers."

I poured the cereal into the bowl. There was no sense in arguing. "Sure. Whatever."

"Good. I'll make some phone calls."

We went at the cabinets with crowbars. It was pretty fun, actually. My dad was really into it—he kept making these crazy war cries.

Later, we lugged out the broken plywood and particle board and tossed it into the dumpster.

My dad was beaming. "Feels good doesn't it?"

"I guess. How's your back?"

"Fine," he said. "Great, in fact." He beat his chest and took in a big breath of air. "Nothing wrong with a little hard work."

"Just be careful," I said.

My dad grinned at me.

That afternoon, the phone rang. My dad yelled out from his bedroom, "I'm not here!"

I yelled back, "Okay!" and picked up the phone. "Hello?"

"Hey Colin." It was Gordie.

"Yeah?"

"There's a party over here."

It sounded like he had already been drinking. Gordie never drank unless it was properly sanctioned.

"That's good," I said.

"Want to come?"

"Where? The lab?"

"Yeah. Know where it is?"

"No."

"You going to come?"

"If you give me directions."

"What? Oh, right." After telling me how to get there, he said, "Hey Colin."

"What?"

There was a pause. "Never mind. I'll tell you later."

"Alright. Tell me later."

Stanford is a strange place. All the buildings match. It's like some kind of theme park—like Disneyland or something.

The whole place is permit-only parking, so I parked the Barracuda off campus and walked in through a long corridor of palm trees.

Behind the Stanford medical center there's a huge

network of labs and research facilities—basically a bunch of double-wide trailers dressed up with nice paint jobs and neatly-lettered plaques. There were several big generators going full tilt. It was pretty noisy.

Finally, I found the place—another double-wide with a sign that said: MOLECULAR ENDOCRINOLOGY.

I pushed through the door and walked into what looked like the main room, with a couple of folding tables and a few scattered chairs. There was a keg in the middle of the floor and a bunch of acne-ridden science guys were standing around in lab coats drinking beer from plastic cups.

Gordie practically ran up to me. "They got a keg," he said, all proud.

"I can see that."

"They do this on the last Friday of every month. It's a tradition."

"Tradition is good."

We walked over to the keg. I got my own cup and started pumping. I was looking around. I didn't see any women.

Some short guy walked up to us. He stuck his hand out at me.

"Hi, I'm Jon. No H."

"No what?"

"No H," he said.

"In his name," Gordie said. "No H in his name."

I shook the guy's hand. "No H. Got it."

The guy was just kind of smiling at me, so I turned to Gordie, who was giggling. "Where do you guys butcher the rats?"

"I'll show you," Gordie said.

I followed Gordie into a windowless room with a row of giant refrigerators and a long table. Toward the end of the table was a small stainless-steel device. It looked kind of like a garlic press.

"That's the guillotine?" I said.

"That's it."

It looked like it had a pretty sharp blade. I put my hand on the handle and pressed down.

"Smooth action," I said. Then I said, "Come here."

"What?"

"Just come here."

Gordie walked over to me. "What?"

I pointed at the guillotine. "Put your finger in there," I said.

Gordie just looked at me.

"Come on, you won't feel a thing."

"Fuck you."

"It's for science."

Gordie didn't seem to think it was funny. I shrugged, took a sip of my beer. "So where's the big shot?"

"You mean Dr. Weisman?"

"Yeah. I want to meet him."

"He's at a conference in Nice."

I nodded. The fluorescent light was starting to get to me. And the smell. There was a bad, chemical smell.

Then Gordie said, "I really like Beth."

"Oh yeah?"

"Yeah. She came by the other night, when you were up in San Francisco. We talked for a long time."

"Oh," I said. "So that's what you wanted to tell me?"

"What?"

"That's what you wanted to tell me—before, on the phone?"

"Oh yeah." he said. "Yeah, she's really cool."

I wondered what Beth thought of Gordie.

"So what about this Dan guy?" Gordie said.

"She told you about him?"

"Not really."

"He's the ex-boyfriend."

"Sounds like a real asshole." Gordie looked serious when he said this—almost angry.

I shrugged.

I stayed for a few more beers. Gordie got pretty wasted—his nose turned bright red. I had to drive him home.

On the way home he kept mumbling about Dan. "The guy sounds like a real asshole," he said.

Fifteen

Andy Warhol made a movie of a shadow creeping slowly across a building, in real time. That was it—that was the whole movie. I saw part of it at a screening at Berkeley. It was something like eight hours long.

My life was about as exciting as that movie. I read the paper, watched TV, ate, did the occasional bit of work when my dad was around. It was boring at first, but it's surprising how fast you can settle into a routine. The no routine routine.

But leaving the house was always an adventure. I wouldn't say that Mountain View was a small town. And I wouldn't say that I knew that many people. But for a while there, I was running into everyone. I'd run into people I had barely talked to in high school and it would be like seeing a long lost friend.

At the hardware store, I ran into this guy, Eric, who I knew from track. Right before we graduated, he put his face through the windshield of his Toyota pickup, and he had some pinkish scars around his eyes. Now he was working construction with his uncle, making good money—he already had a new truck with fat tires and a roll bar. His cart was loaded with charcoal for a party he was having that night, and he invited me over. I could picture some of the people who'd be there—mostly a bunch of morons. I think his crowd included a guy named Travis Lowe who had torched a bunch of people's lockers in middle school, and Jimmy West, who I had heard was getting to be a big-time coke dealer. I told him I'd try to make it.

I ran into Aaron at Safeway. He was kind of an art guy, with the black clothes and silly suede loafers. I knew him from a brief stint with the high school newspaper—probably the stupidest thing I ever signed up for—where he had been one of the photography guys. Now he was in a punk band and was at the Safeway buying roach motels for their practice space. We shook hands and talked for a while, updating each other on the goings on of other high school friends and acquaintances.

The strangest run-in was at the gas station, where I saw Jane Moss. I'd lost my virginity to her on this horrible school ski trip in Tahoe during our junior year—I still remember the cold tile floor of the bathroom in this big cheesy lodge. When Beth found out about it she made fun of me for a year afterwards. Sometimes she would just say "Jane Moss" and start laughing.

Anyway, Jane was gassing up her new white Jeep, a present from her rich parents. I think she had been a disappointment for them, getting stoned every afternoon behind school, flunking classes.

"Hi," she said.

"Hi," I said.

She was wearing ugly gold earrings and a white jeans jacket—I guess to match the Jeep.

"How have you been?"

"Good," I said. "Yourself?"

"Good."

She had a smile frozen on her face. I had no idea what she was thinking. Maybe she was trying to remember who the hell I was.

The pump clicked off. She removed the nozzle and replaced the gas cap.

"It was great seeing you," she said.

"You too," I said.

My father couldn't decide on new cabinets—the few that he liked either ended up being too expensive or they had to be special-ordered and there was a long wait. And then he threw out his back again—this time bending over the sink to brush his teeth. So the cabinet concept was put on hold.

But he had other plans—namely, for a new front lawn. It came in a big rug. Three guys showed up in a truck and rolled it out.

After they left, I lay down in the middle of the grass. The blades were sharp and dark green, and with the sun heating it up, it smelled like plastic. But I liked it—I liked having a real lawn. I knew that the drought would make fast work of it—that soon there would be big yellow patches. But for now it was new and fresh and alive.

A few days later, my mom called.

"Colin," she said.

"Hi Mom."

My father was in the kitchen making himself some kind of healthy fruit concoction in the blender. He had looked nervous when the phone rang, but then he perked up when he heard that it was my mother.

My mom said, "How are things?"

"Fine," I said. "How are you?"

"Good," she said. "Great actually."

My dad made a show of being busy with his shake, adding wheat germ, then some chunky-looking soy stuff. He hit blend.

"So, is your father keeping you busy with the house?"

I could barely hear. I said, "Pretty much."

"Because, what I was wondering... I was wondering when you could come visit. I thought that maybe we should set a date. Otherwise, these things have a habit of just slipping away."

"Oh, right."

My father started trying to pour his fruit shake into a glass. It was too thick—it wouldn't come out of the blender.

"So what do you think?"

"I don't know. Yeah, maybe."

"Maybe... what?"

I said, "Maybe I can come visit. Yeah."

My dad turned the blender upside down and started shaking.

"Colin, I was asking when you can come visit. Maybe it was wrong of me, but I was assuming that you could, in fact, visit your mother."

The fruit shake shot out of the blender and fell on the floor. My father said, "Shit."

I was trying not to laugh.

My mother said, "Colin?"

"Yeah?"

My dad was looking down at his shake. Then he said, "Can I talk to her a second?"

"Dad wants to talk to you," I said.

"What? He's there?" My mother sighed. "Put him on, I guess."

I handed my father the phone, then stepped outside. I didn't want to hear their conversation—I didn't want to hear my father's side of it, that is. My father was really annoying with my mom—obsequious and pestering and manipulative all at the same time.

It was a pretty nice day out, and the back patio was hot in the sun. Before my mom moved out, she used to like to sunbathe out here. She had this lime green bathing suit leftover from the sixties and she'd lie out on this reclining lawn chair (which was now in the dumpster) and sometimes she'd flirt with the previous Corvette-driving neighbor across the fence. She'd often be out here when I came home for school, and she'd try to make me put suntan lotion on her back. That always freaked me out.

So I was thinking about my mom and my imminent trip to Arizona when I noticed our new neighbor standing in his backyard. At first I thought he was holding a walkie-talkie. Then I saw that it was the remote control for a small model helicopter. I watched as the helicopter lifted off from the middle of his lawn and floated over the top of his house. The tail rotor clipped a telephone line and the helicopter crashed onto his roof. It thrashed around for a moment like a dying insect before sliding off the roof and dropping into the bushes below.

I could hear my father calling for me inside the house. I stepped around the side of the garage, where he wouldn't be able to see me. Just over the fence, my neighbor was mumbling to himself about his downed helicopter. I held my breath.

I kept going back and forth on whether or not to call Chloe. There were several Andersons in the phone book, but I was pretty sure Chloe's family would be the ones on Broadway—in Pacific Heights, a wealthy neighborhood of San Francisco. I could almost picture it—one of those big houses overlooking the Bay. I imagined a wrought iron gate and a big circular driveway, security cameras and uniformed servants dusting the curtains.

Finally, I called. It rang a few times and then someone—a woman, probably Chloe's mother—answered. "Hello?"

I could hear people laughing in the background. Probably her boyfriend's entire family was there, visiting.

I hung up.

Gwen came by one night and knocked on the door. My dad yelled, "I'm not here!" and shut his bedroom door.

I opened the door. Gwen was standing there, wearing a rumpled brown dress. It looked like a bag.

"He's not here."

"Don't lie to me Colin."

I shrugged. What could I say?

"Can I come in?"

"No," I said.

"Why not?"

"We had a toxic spill?"

She pushed past me.

In a moment, she was at my father's door. "I know you're in there."

No answer.

"Open up, I just want to talk."

No answer.

"Please?" She slid down the door. She was weeping.

I went into the living room. Gordie was watching TV.

"What's going on?" Gordie said.

"Nothing," I said. "Could you turn up the volume?"

A few days later, Beth invited me and Gordie over to her mom's house to watch a movie. Beth's mom was at her boyfriend's place, so it was just the three of us in the house, sitting on their overstuffed couches.

We were in the middle of the opening credits when the doorbell rang. Of course, I knew who it would be.

Beth went to the door. When he heard Dan's voice, Gordie started getting all puffed up. I told him to relax, let Beth handle it.

Then the yelling started.

Gordie said, "Come on." He got up. I followed.

Dan was drunk, standing in the glare of the porch light in his standard outfit of slip-on Vans and a Mexican hoodie. His Camaro was pulled up part-way on the sidewalk. I couldn't believe what a fucking cliché all this was.

I was stuck behind Gordie in this narrow hallway, next to a tall mirror and all of Beth's mom's knickknacks—little porcelain figures and Venetian glass.

Dan spotted me. "Colin?" he said. He shook his head like he was disappointed.

Beth said, "Could you please leave now?"

"Oh come on. I just want to talk to you."

"Maybe she doesn't want to talk to you," Gordie said.

I rolled my eyes.

"Yeah? And who the FUCK are you?"

I said, "Beth, just close the door." But I knew she wouldn't. She enjoyed the dramatics, the attention. Lights went on across the street.

Gordie pushed forward, into the spotlight. "Why don't you go home?" he said.

"Who the hell is this guy?"

Dan was pleading with Beth, with me—I think he could see what was going to happen as clearly as I could.

But Gordie was stupid. He said, "A friend. And I think you should leave."

The punch was pretty half-assed—it kind of grazed Gordie's cheek. But Gordie went down.

Dan looked embarrassed all of a sudden. "Shit," he said.

Beth pushed him away, knelt down to Gordie.

"Alright, Dan," I said. "You happy?"

"No." He was like a sullen baby.

"Well, could you leave now?" I said.

"Fuck you, Colin. Fuck you." But he started walking back to his car.

"Gordie," Beth said. "Are you okay?"

Gordie was looking up at her. I swear to God he was smiling. It was pathetic.

Dan pulled away with the necessary screeching and smoking of tires.

Gordie said, "My neck."

Beth set Gordie up with a ridiculous neck brace—duct taping a towel around his neck—and then we watched the rest of the movie.

I glanced over at Gordie a few times during the movie. He looked all smug and proud.

Sixteen

My birthday is on the Fourth of July. It was pretty exciting when I was a kid, until I figured out that all the firecrackers weren't for me.

The morning of the Fourth, my sister called to wish me a happy birthday. She also called to announce that she was coming to visit a few days later.

"Brad has a meeting out there, and I decided to come along and bring the kids. I haven't seen you or Dad in almost a year." I heard the click for call waiting. "Well, I should go. I'll call again when I know more."

Gordie had started hanging out with Jon no H. Turns out he was heavily into Tai Chi. He was also heavily into juggling and bongos. And he knew a whole bunch of people who were into Tai Chi, juggling and bongos. So he converted Gordie—to the Tai Chi stuff, anyway. You didn't need any equipment for that.

So most mornings, Gordie would wake up early to go do Tai Chi out on the Stanford lawns. And on weekends, Jon no H would show up in his battered Celica and they would drive up to San Francisco, where the hard-core juggling, bongo-playing Tai Chi people lived. He picked

Gordie up again on the morning of my birthday for what was supposed to be a full day of this stuff. I could see the bongos stacked up against the back window as they drove away.

That night, Jack and Beth came over. The two of them had a strange and vaguely antagonistic relationship. Jack really hated Dan—once, they had come close to blows over a comment Dan had made about Jack's shaved legs. Beth and Jack hadn't really seen much of each other over the last few years. So it was kind of nice, both of them hanging out and getting along for my benefit on my birthday.

Jack brought over a six pack and a bottle of Jack Daniel's. We sat in my kitchen, took shots and chased them with beer.

Beth winced after taking a shot. "Disgusting."

Jack laughed. Then he said, "So he's finally nineteen."

"Old," I said.

"You're such a lagger," Beth said. She and Jack were both nineteen already.

"So where are my presents?" I said.

"You don't get any," Jack said.

"What do you mean?" Beth said. "He gets to hang out with us." Then she said, "No, I got you something, silly."

She pulled out a flat-looking box.

"Looks like a shirt," Jack said.

Beth said, "Just let him open it."

I opened it.

Jack started laughing. "It is a shirt."

"What?" Beth said. "Shut up."

I held it up. It was a button-up short sleeve shirt with some kind of floral pattern. "I like it."

"I saw it and thought of you."

Jack started laughing again. Beth punched him. "You're such a shit," she said.

I pulled off my t-shirt and put on the new shirt.

"See?" Beth said. "It looks good on you."

"Thanks, Beth," I said.

"You're very welcome." She glared at Jack.

"Here, I got you something," Jack said. He pulled a bunch of bottle rockets out of his bag and tossed them to me.

"Nice," I said.

"Oh, firecrackers," Beth said. "Very mature. How old are you? Ten?"

"Twelve," Jack said.

After a few more shots we went out to the front yard to fire bottle rockets at cars. We used Beth as a spotter—she stood behind a tree and called out when she saw headlights. We fired them from the side of the garage.

The cars were few and far between and we weren't having much luck hitting any.

"This is the last one," Jack said.

"Here comes one," Beth yelled.

Jack lit the bottle rocket.

"Never mind, it's turning," Beth said.

"Fuck," Jack said. He turned around and shot it into a tree. It got lodged in a branch and just kind of sputtered.

"You trying to set the tree on fire?" Beth said.

"Yes," Jack said. He walked over to the base of the tree and held a lighter to it. "It's not catching," he said.

"Be patient," I said.

Just then, a police car pulled up in front of the house. The window rolled down. Jack walked out to see what was up. He had a lot of confidence when it came to cops—his uncle was a cop in Sacramento, and Jack always had an easy time with them.

He talked to them for about a minute and then they drove away.

I said, "What did they want?"

"Said they had a report of some kids shooting bottle rockets."

"Imagine that," Beth said.

We went back inside. Beth looked at the bottle of Jack Daniel's, which was pretty low. "Did we really drink that much?"

"Yeah," Jack said. "And Colin has to finish it."

"What?" I said. "No thanks."

Jack poured more shots. "Come on. Drink up."

"Peer pressure," I said. Jack and I each took another shot.

Beth shook her head and opened a beer. Then she said, "So I hear you have a new girlfriend. An older woman."

No one said anything for a moment. Then Jack said, "Who? Me?"

Beth said, "You."

Jack shrugged. "Yeah."

"Well?" Beth said.

"Well what?"

"I don't know, what's she like?"

"She's nice."

"Nice? Is that all you can say?"

Jack shrugged. "I don't know."

"Is she cute?"

Jack shrugged.

"She's a babe," I said.

"Really?" Beth said.

Jack smiled but didn't say anything.

"Okay, okay," Beth said. "We don't have to talk about her."

Jack pulled the last beer from the six pack. He got up to throw the plastic six-pack holder in the trash.

"Wait," Beth said.

"What?"

She got some scissors off the kitchen counter and cut the plastic into pieces. Then she threw it out.

Jack said, "Why'd you do that?"

"They strangle fish."

Jack laughed. "What?"

"Most garbage ends up in the ocean. Then fish or birds or whatever get stuck in them and die."

Jack looked at me.

I shrugged. "It's true."

Jack shook his head and sat down. "I guess they teach this stuff in college."

"No," Beth said. "Everyone knows that. Except you I guess."

"Oh," Jack said. "Right."

After that, no one said anything. The refrigerator clicked on with a hum.

"Well this is exciting," Beth said.

I yawned. "Damn exciting."

"It's just not the same without Rat Boy," Jack said.

"Yeah," Beth said. "Where is he, anyway?"

"In San Francisco with some of his new bongo buddies."

Beth giggled. "Well, I wish he was here. He's so...funny."

Jack laughed. "The guy's a dork."

"That's not very nice," Beth said.

"True though," Jack said.

"You guys are mean."

"What?" I said. "I didn't say anything."

"Yeah, but you didn't defend him, either."

"He doesn't need defending," I said. "'Cept maybe from you."

Beth pretended to look shocked. "And what is that supposed to mean?"

I turned to Jack. "Beth likes to toy with Gordie."

"Do not," she said.

"Yeah you do," I said. "And if you're not careful, you're going to break his heart."

"Whatever," Beth said.

Jack was the first to leave—he always got tired really fast. One minute he'd be full of energy and the next minute he'd have this blank stare on his face.

After he left, Beth said, "Jack seems different."

"He does?" I said.

"Yeah. More quiet or something."

I thought about this for a second——maybe it was true. Then again, Beth always thought that Jack was full of himself—I think because she knew he wasn't interested in her. I shrugged. "Maybe."

She yawned. "Maybe it's just me. Maybe I'm just tired and drunk."

"That could be it," I said.

Then she said, "You don't really think I'm toying with Gordie?"

"A bit."

"I'm just trying to be nice. What's wrong with that?"

"Nothing," I said. "Nothing at all."

Beth pretended to pout. Then she stood up and stretched. "Well, happy birthday." She looked at her watch. "Oops, it's not your birthday any more."

"Damn. Really?"

"Really. Now you're nineteen and one hour old."

I smiled. "Thanks for the shirt."

She gave me a quick kiss on the cheek. "No problemo."

I was about to go to bed when Gordie called.

"Hello?" I said.

"Colin?"

"Gordie?" I said. "Where are you?"

As it turned out, Gordie and a few of his Tai Chi buddies had ended up at some strip club in the Tenderloin. Gordie had refused to go in—he had decided to wait for them at a cafe across the street. Apparently, a few hours had gone by and everyone was still in there.

"So, what, this was some kind of Tai Chi field trip?"

"No," Gordie said. "Just Jon and this guy Eric."

"Who's Eric?"

"Never mind."

I heard someone say something in the background. There was a muffled sound. Then Gordie came back on.

"What was that?" I said.

"Some guy asked me what time it is."

I laughed. I could picture him on the dark sidewalk, huddled up to the pay phone.

I said, "So what are you going to do?"

"I don't know. What should I do?"

"Well, it's too late for the train."

There was a gap, a clicking noise. Gordie said, "Shit, I'm out of change."

More clicking, then silence. I said, "Good luck," but I doubt he heard me.

After that, I lay in bed, drunk. I could still hear the occasional pop of a firecracker. July Fourth had always marked the middle of the summer for me. And it marked the beginning of the slow slide back toward school. But this summer seemed longer somehow, seemed different.

Since I had gone to Berkeley, I had started having trouble seeing very far into the future. As a kid, you are taught to see life as a series of steps. One step logically leads to another—school, job, marriage, kids, blah, blah, blah. I had never really bought into that, but still, up to now, life had seemed like a fairly logical progression. In other words, there were always things I knew I had to get through. It seemed like I was always waiting for one thing to end so the next thing could start. And I'd always had this nagging, impatient feeling.

The problem was, I still had that nagging, impatient feeling, but it was confusing because I didn't feel like I was waiting for anything to start. Berkeley was just two months away, but it didn't have that weird, beckoning power that every other new school year always seemed to have. I felt indifferent. Indifferent but vaguely impatient at the same time.

I dreamt about painting the house. It was one of those dreams where I couldn't control anything. The paint had a mind of its own—it spread across the walls, changing color as it went, like a bad 60s tie-dye. Plus, the can was leaking, and the floor was a big sticky mess.

When I dream, I always feel like I'm right on the edge of figuring out that I'm having a dream—all kinds of weird shit might be happening, but somewhere in the back of my mind I always know that it's not real, that none of it really matters.

In any case, I normally don't remember my dreams— that is, unless I wake up in the middle of them. Which is what happened. I was trying to soak up all the paint with a bunch of bath towels, and then I was being shaken awake.

"Colin, wake up."

"Wha..?" I opened my eyes but I could barely see. It was dark. Then my eyes focused and I saw that it was Gordie.

"Colin, I need some money."

I sat up. "What?"

"I need fifty dollars."

I saw then that there was someone else in the room. "Who's that?"

"It's the cab driver."

The guy was short and stocky, probably in his fifties—he looked like a scruffy version of my high school chemistry teacher.

"You took a cab?" I said. "From San Francisco?"

"I didn't know what else to do. I'd get the money from my ATM but I'm overdrawn and I don't get paid 'til next week.'"

"Can we hurry this up a bit?" the cab driver said. "I don't have all night here."

I got out of bed and picked my pants up off the floor. I pulled out my wallet. "I have twenty," I said. "That's all."

"Twenty's not gonna do it," the driver said. He looked at his watch. "I'm giving you two minutes"

"Then what?" I said.

The driver didn't say anything.

I handed Gordie my twenty. "Can I go back to bed now?"

Gordie looked at the cab driver, as if for approval. The cab driver made no sign one way or another.

"Alright," I said. "Hold on a second."

I walked out of my room and down the hall to my dad's bedroom. The spittoon still had a ton of change in it—mostly nickels and dimes and pennies, but there was at least another thirty dollars' worth in there. I lifted the spittoon and walked down the hall.

"Here you go," I said, and handed it to the driver. "Keep the change."

"What's this?"

"All my money."

He frowned.

"Go ahead, count it," I said. "There's more than enough there, I'm sure."

"I don't have to take this."

"Yes you do," I said. "It's legal tender."

As we watched the driver walk out the front door with my dad's spittoon, I said, "Well, you owe me a lot of Mexican food."

Gordie said, "Fine."

"You're welcome," I said. And then I went back to bed.

Seventeen

Then, somehow, I managed to get sick. First I got one of those sore throats where you feel like you swallowed something wrong, then I got that stoned/punched in the head feeling and my nose started running like a faucet. I spent a lot of time lying in my bed, throwing wadded-up toilet paper on the floor.

Getting sick in the summer is weird. When you get sick in the winter it makes sense—the weather sucks, and lots of other people are sick, too. But when you get sick in the summer, it's confusing. It's sunny and warm and everyone else is healthy. You feel stupid.

Since I had returned home, I hadn't really been spending much time in my room. It was still piled with crap, and it smelled musty—I think there must have been a leak in the roof over the winter. My dresser had gotten all warped somehow—you couldn't close any of the drawers, and the laminated coating was peeling off the side. It was depressing.

I hadn't changed any of the posters or done anything to the room since I was about twelve. I had a Pink Floyd poster that I had put up in middle school and a Ferrari poster that must have dated back to fourth grade. It was all incredibly lame, but for some reason, I'd left it all in place.

My sister's room was even more of a time warp. A few days before, I'd finally gotten around to clearing it out so we could move Gordie in there. Her stuff had been obscured by the boxes of my dad's stuff—most of which went into the dumpster. But under all that crap, there was my sister's room—and it was still pretty much the way she left it before she went off to college. There was her bed with the purple bedspread, and her night table with the little drawer that she always used to keep locked (there was nothing left in it, other than a bunch of yellowed Garfield cartoons which she had clipped out of the newspaper). And then there was the little green bench which was lined with her huge collection of stuffed animals. I recognized all of them—the generic ones like Curious George and Winnie the Poo mixed in the oddball teddy bears and other animals. Her favorite had been Squirrel, who was made out of faded blue corduroy, and who was missing an eye—the corduroy was still dark blue where the eye had been.

It had already been seven years since she had moved out—seven years since she went off to college. It was weird being six years apart. I knew that I was an accident—I knew that they tried to have a second kid a short while after my sister and they couldn't. Then, six years later, I showed up.

My sister could remember a whole other life before we got to California. I was born in Denver but I don't remember it—it's just a name: Denver. My first memory is of splashing around in a baby pool in the backyard in the California sunshine.

I hadn't seen my sister all that much since she had left. But it's not like my sister and I ever really hung out when I was little—she was more like my babysitter. And then, before I knew it, she was out of there—first to LA, and then off to the East Coast. It was like she'd had an escape plan. She always said that she didn't plan to go that far away, but the truth is, I think she saw what was coming with my parents and she wanted to get as far away as possible. I was oblivious, or in denial or something.

So she was already gone by the time my mom moved out. I was thirteen at the time—my voice had just cracked and I was getting my first zits—and I still remember the day they told me. I had started taking tennis lessons a few weeks before, and I had just come back from the club. I had this new tennis ball pressurizer my mom had bought for me. It was made of clear plastic and had a little hand pump. I had three new green balls in there.

They were waiting for me when I came home. I don't remember what they said exactly, I just remember their faces—they were terrified, guilty. They started making all sorts of promises and guarantees. It made me feel vaguely ill, vaguely dizzy, and once they were done talking—or once they seemed to be done—I asked if I could go to the bathroom. I didn't have to piss or anything. I just wanted to get away from them, and going to my room would seem too wimpy.

I went into the bathroom and shut the door. I paced

around a bit and then I sat down on the toilet. I still had the ball pressurizer. I started pumping it up. I thought maybe if I kept pumping, the balls would implode—like if you took it down to the bottom of the ocean in a submarine and then threw them out the porthole. But it was pumped up pretty much all the way and nothing seemed to be happening. I let out the air with a hiss.

I could hear my mom and dad talking. They were probably discussing how it went. Then my mom was at the door. "Colin, are you okay?"

"Yeah," I said. And I don't know why—I guess I wanted it to seem like I was actually doing something in there—but I stood up, opened the lid of the toilet and dropped one of the balls into the bowl. It plopped into the water and just floated there. A floater. I flushed the toilet. It swirled around, bobbed, and then went down. I couldn't believe it. It made this glunk, glunk, glunk sound as it went down the pipe.

I couldn't wait for the bowl to fill up again. I put in another ball and flushed. Same thing—glunk, glunk, glunk.

My dad said, "Colin, what are you doing?"

"Nothing," I said. I was waiting for the bowl to fill again.

The third time the bowl flowed over massively—somehow this caught me by surprise and soaked my new white tennis shoes. Water flowed everywhere, soaking the small bathroom rug. When I opened the door, the water spilled out into the hallway. My parents were just standing there. My mother said, "Oh honey," and the way she said it—I mean, up to then, I was doing okay, and with the tennis balls, I had almost forgotten—I started crying like a baby. Later I really regretted that—regretted giving them any reaction.

So I was thinking about all this weird shit as I lay in my room, sick. It probably sounds melodramatic as hell, but I guess those stupid posters represented the last time I'd really given a shit about something like decorating my room—the last time I'd really cared about the house or what went on inside it. After that, I didn't even care enough to take all that stuff down.

I was finally getting over my cold—I was just getting into the thick green gob phase—when my sister called again.

She called from a hotel in San Jose. Supposedly, they were only going to be in town for a day before heading down to LA to visit some friends. Anyway, she wanted me to pick up dad and bring him over.

My sister didn't like being alone with our dad—she said it was awkward, that they always ended up talking about mom. She liked to have me around—she said I was a good buffer.

My dad had seemed pretty distracted lately. He had started spending the occasional night back at the duplex with Gwen. I didn't know what was going on and I didn't want to ask, either.

I drove over and picked him up at his new office—it was over in some kind of mall complex, he had to give me directions. He came out with this little inflatable back pillow. When he got in the car, he wedged it behind his back.

He looked around his seat. "Where are the seatbelts?"

"1964. Remember?"

"I remember 1964. And I remember seatbelts."

"Nope. Not mandatory until 1968."

"That right?"

"Yeah, and steering columns weren't collapsible until 1969."

"So this car is a death trap."

"Unsafe at any speed."

My dad put his pillow against the dashboard. "There. It's an airbag."

In the hotel elevator, my dad bent down to tie his shoe. He got kind of stuck like that. I had to hold the door when we got to my sister's floor.

"You okay?"

He pulled himself back up using the chrome railing. "Fine," he said.

We walked down a long hallway. There were little lights every five yards or so.

My dad said, "What number is it again?"

"I thought you knew the number."

"What?" My dad stopped in his tracks. He never knew when I was joking. Sometimes I didn't know when I was joking.

"It's right here." I knocked.

My sister opened the door. Her kids—Justin and Sara, ages two and three—were right behind her. There were plastic toys everywhere—red, yellow and blue.

My sister looked tired. "Hi Dad. Hi Colin."

Justin ran out into the hallway. He took off down the hall.

"Jailbreak," I said.

The three of us sat on the bed while the kids played on the floor. There was a little vent along the bottom of the floor blowing cold air. It made the curtains billow.

My sister was wearing one of those loose-fitting pregnancy dresses. I guess she was already in her eighth month. She still wore her hair long with bangs in front—the same basic look she'd had since she was fourteen. And I don't know if it was because she was pregnant or what, but her nose and ears were red. It looked like she'd been out in the cold or something.

My dad was staring at the bed pattern—orange and brown hexagons. "How much is this place a night?"

"I don't know. Brad's company is paying."

My dad wrinkled his nose. "That air they're pumping in here is probably recycled. We should open the window."

"Tried already. They're sealed shut."

Justin got up and marched into the bathroom. A few seconds later his sister followed.

"Are we going to see Brad?" I said.

"I kind of doubt it. He's got wall to wall meetings."

"That sucks."

"I know. He's been very busy lately. We're hoping he's going to get a promotion."

We heard screaming from the bathroom.

"I'm going to go see what those kids are up to," my dad said.

My sister smiled as he disappeared into the bathroom.

"So," she said.

"So."

"Did you get a haircut?"

"What?" I said. "Since I saw you last?"

She laughed. "Okay, stupid question." Then she said, "I'm glad you guys could come by."

"Me, too," I said.

"I realized when I got here that I forgot your present."

"That's okay."

"It's all wrapped and everything. I'll mail it to you when I get back."

"Cool."

My sister smiled. "So, what are you up to these days?"

"Not a whole lot."

"No?"

I shrugged.

"So you're nineteen."

"That's right."

She just shook her head. "My little brother. My baby little brother."

"What the hell?" I said.

"I just can't believe how old you are now."

"Yeah," I said. "Well look at you, mom."

She smiled. "Scary isn't it?"

Just then there was a crash, followed by screaming. Justin came running out of the bathroom.

My father emerged a second later. He said, "I think he bumped his head on the toilet."

"Let me see," she said.

My dad and I watched as she took Justin in her arms and kissed him on the head. He immediately stopped crying.

"He's fine," she said. "He has a hard head like his father."

On the drive back, my dad said, "Those are some cute kids."

"Yup," I said.

My dad said, "Your sister seems happy."

"She does."

For some reason I was thinking about this boyfriend my sister had for a while in high school. Ted. He was a tuba player in the marching band—nice, but kind of a geek. She dumped him pretty quick. I think I liked him more than she did—I definitely used him, taking full advantage of the fact that he was trying to ingratiate himself with my sister. And I continued to get him to drive me around after they broke up, until he figured out that my sister wasn't going to take him back.

So what if my sister had ended up with Ted the tuba player? I didn't have anything against Brad or anything. But my sister had met Brad at a different time in her life. And somehow, because I wasn't around my sister at that time—because I didn't know her as well then, didn't know all the things that were important to her—it made it seem like I knew her less well now. Maybe that doesn't make any sense.

My father was thinking, too. After a while he said, "Your mother was happy when you guys were that age, too. I think so, anyway."

I realized that he was looking at me. I said, "Yeah, she was." But what the hell did I know?

My dad shook his head. "Time flies."

Eighteen

"You know what I want?" Beth said. "You know what I've been thinking about all morning?"

"What?" I said.

"Cotton candy."

Beth and Gordie had both taken the day off from work. The three of us had piled into the Barracuda, and were headed for Santa Cruz. Gordie was sitting up front—he had a problem with car sickness. He was wearing these goofy Bermuda shorts. His skinny, hairy legs were butt white.

Gordie said, "I've never had cotton candy."

"You've never had cotton candy?" Beth said.

"So?" Gordie said.

"So?" Beth said. "That's lame."

"You haven't missed much," I said.

"Yes. He. Has," Beth said, emphasizing each word by poking me in the back of the head. "You'll see," she said to Gordie.

It was a forty-minute drive to Santa Cruz. Beth spent most of it putting on suntan lotion, and she kept jamming her knees into the back of my seat. I just tried to focus on the road—Highway 17, a winding four-lane highway with a cement divider and a gravel shoulder—keeping one eye on the temperature gauge.

I've always liked the Santa Cruz Beach Boardwalk because it's open. You can buy tickets to individual rides and not get sucked into paying for a day pass. Because no matter how excited you might be about an amusement park beforehand, if you're not a little kid, you're going to be sick of the whole concept after a few rides.

When we got there, Beth made a beeline for the cotton candy. She bought a big blue one for herself and a big pink one for Gordie. Gordie tasted it and made a face, then offered the rest to me. When I declined, he tossed his in the trash, which really pissed off Beth.

Santa Cruz is famous mostly for the Big Dipper, a huge rickety wooden roller coaster with peeling paint and ancient, creaking cars. We had to practically drag Gordie onto it, but he ended up really liking it, screaming like a maniac before every drop. It was a good place to start, because after that he trusted us. We were going to need that trust to get him on the Rock-O-Plane.

Basically, the Rock-O-Plane is a really sick version of a ferris wheel—the difference being that you ride in a fully enclosed metal cage, and there is a lever you can use to lock out the hub. That lever is the key—if you don't touch it, you'll have a pretty straightforward and boring ferris wheel-type ride. But if, as you crest the top, you pull the lever, the hub will lock and you'll go into the descent upside-down—and face first. And with the whole park rushing up at you, you'll be thrown onto the top (now the bottom) of the cage like a hamster who's lost his footing on the exercise wheel. The blood floods to your head and you see stars. It's painful, it makes you feel sick, but it's also funny as hell.

Two people fit in a cage, and so the ride always turns into a fight over the stick. Controlling the stick doesn't lessen the punishment, but being able to inflict the pain seems to mitigate your own discomfort. Beth had made me promise not to tell Gordie anything about the Rock-O-Plane. She wanted to break Gordie in on it. The poor guy didn't know what he was getting into.

As usual, there was no line. I think Gordie realized that something was up, but he was in a good mood after the Big Dipper, and he wasn't going to back down in front of Beth. Beth and Gordie got in one cage, and I got into the one right behind them.

There was some more loading and unloading before the ride started. People rocked their cages back and forth in anticipation. The Pacific Ocean spread out for miles and miles. I was directly below Gordie and Beth—I could see their feet on the bottom of the cage.

The ride started with a lurch. Up we went. As we crested the top, Beth locked the hub. Their cage tilted forward, and I heard Gordie start screaming like a little girl. I followed, locking the hub on my own cage—mostly so I could keep an eye on their cage. Gordie was still screaming as we swung through the bottom of the arc—his hands were pressed against the inside of the cage. And as we crested the top again, he started to beg. But Beth had no mercy.

At the end of the ride, Gordie practically collapsed on the pavement.

"What? I said. "You didn't like it?"

Beth was trying not to laugh. She bit her lower lip and shook her head.

We got some hot dogs and went down to the beach. The sun was hot but there was a good breeze going. We found a spot near the water and Beth took off her shoes and wriggled her toes in the sand.

There were a lot of people out there—teenagers and families with children. A few yards away, a young-looking mother was changing her kid's diapers. We were definitely downwind from the operation.

To be honest, I'm not a real beach person. I'm not into sunbathing and you can only stare out at the water for so long without getting bleary-eyed.

When Beth finished her hot dog, she flopped over on her stomach. "Who wants to give me a back rub?"

Gordie looked at me.

"What are you looking at me for?" I said.

"I wasn't looking at you." Gordie's face was bright red.

I was sick of Beth and her games, of Gordie and his pathetic crush.

"So why don't you give her a back rub?" I got up and walked away.

I heard Gordie say, "What's his problem?"

Beth said, "He's just jealous."

I walked farther down the beach. Two hippies were

flying kites—big Chinese dragons with teeth and long tails. The wind was really making the kites zip around the place, and the hippies were having trouble controlling them. Finally, they got tangled up with each other and crashed onto the beach—almost hitting a group of dogs that were circling around, sniffing each other's butts.

Beth's words were ringing in my ears. "He's just jealous." It made me angry. But jealous wasn't the right word—I mean, I knew that Beth was just toying with Gordie, so how could I be jealous? It was more like this: watching Gordie flail around Beth was like watching a sad, pathetic version of myself. I guess I thought that in the nine months or so since I'd seen her that I'd changed, that I'd toughened up, gotten cool. But now, all the old feelings were coming back. Beth still had power over me and it pissed me off.

The drive home was quiet. The wind and the sun had made us all pretty dull.

We were half-way home on Highway 17 when Gordie sat up and puked into his hands. Then, in a panic, he started to open the door before I could pull over. The wind threw vomit back onto Beth.

"Gross!" Beth yelled.

When I stopped the car, Gordie jumped out. He leaned over the concrete barrier and puked some more. I turned and watched the steady stream of headlights in the rear-view mirror.

Beth was muttering, trying to wipe barf chunks off her pants. I handed back Gordie's sweatshirt.

"Thanks," she said.

Finally, Gordie finished and got back in the car.

"All better?" I said.

Gordie didn't answer. I pulled back into traffic.

I rolled my window down so I wouldn't have to smell puke. I just wanted to get home.

We got off Highway 17 and merged onto 280. And that's when the Barracuda died. All the lights came on and the engine cut out—along with the power steering. I wrestled the car over to the side of the road.

No one said anything. I sat there for a second. Then I got out.

There is nothing worse than standing alongside a California highway at night, backed up against a cement wall with drivers careening past four cars abreast. I was standing amid the debris—re-treads, smashed batteries and cigarette butts, underwear and shoes. It was too easy to imagine what would happen if someone let their car wander a second. You see that shit all the time—a car drifting onto the shoulder before the driver corrects.

I opened the hood, but it was dark, and anyway I had no idea what was wrong. Something electrical.

Beth got out. "What happened?"

"Fuck if I know."

Beth smiled sweetly. "Should I call a tow truck?"

I shrugged. "Sure."

That's one thing about Beth—she never really freaks out. Even in tense situations, she's always able to maintain a sense of humor.

I went around to the trunk, found a couple of flares—thank you, Mike—and lit them. Then I got back in the car, shutting the door on the noise outside. The flares made this pinkish smoke that drifted around in the night air.

I watched as Beth calmly walked one-hundred yards to the emergency phone. She was still barefoot—for whatever reason—and oblivious to the cars rushing past. After a while she hung up the receiver and tip-toed back to the car.

I had pulled up right against the barrier, so she walked up to the front of the car, waited for a break in the traffic, and then ran and jumped right on top of me. She squirmed over the front seat and fell into the back seat.

"They said about fifteen minutes."

Gordie was dozing—his head pressed against the door window. All of a sudden he sat up and looked around. "What's going on?" he said.

"Nothing," I said. "Go back to sleep."

I remember seeing car wrecks when I was a kid. We'd be on vacation and our parents would tell us not to look—but of course we did, peeking through our fingers, catching glimpses of smashed-up cars, glimpses of people walking around draped with blankets. I remember once seeing an upside-down car, kids' toys strewn across the road, my mother sucking in her breath and saying, "Oh God."

It seems like a strange way to die. Sudden and violent. I imagine it happening in slow motion—there's that moment of recognition, that split second where you see it coming—and then the sudden, hard jerk against the seat belt, the car buckling, and your body being thrown around like clothes in a washing machine.

Beth let out a big yawn, interrupting my dark roadside thoughts. Then she said, "Having a good summer?"

I turned around. She was all curled up in the back seat.

"Great," I said. "You?"

She smiled sleepily. "Fine. Perfect." She yawned again.

Just then a beat-up van pulled over in front of us. The reverse lights went on and I was looking at the little dancing bears on the bumper as he backed up to us. A scraggly-looking guy got out.

"Jesus," Beth said. "It's Charles Manson."

"You folks need some help?" The guy leaned over us, peering into the car. He had a rash on the side of his neck.

"Nope," I said. "Thanks."

"What seems to be the problem?"

Beth mumbled, "None of your fucking business you fucking freak."

I tried to be nice. "Car died. We got a tow truck on the way."

"Triple A?"

Beth sat up. This time, she was louder. "We're fine, thank you."

The guy looked at Beth, then back at me. Then he shrugged and went back to his van.

Beth said, "What a fucking creep."

"Just a good Samaritan," I said.

"Good Samaritan rapist."

The guy started up the van and pulled away.

"But you'd defend me, right Colin?"

"That's Gordie's department."

Gordie woke up again, looking kind of dazed. "What?"

Beth laughed.

The tow truck showed up an hour later. The driver had the baseball cap, the blue shirt with "Jim" embroidered on the pocket. He asked some basic questions, checked a few boxes on his clipboard, then hooked up the car.

Beth and I climbed into the cab. We left Gordie—still asleep—in the car.

Beth dozed lightly on my shoulder. I closed my eyes and listened to the voice of the dispatcher as we drove through the darkness.

Nineteen

My mother FedExed me a plane ticket—I had to sign for it and everything. So there was no way to get out of it. But it was only for three days. I figured I could do three days.

My dad took me to the airport in the Porsche. He pulled into a no-stopping zone. Immediately, a security guard started blowing a whistle at him.

"Say hi to Dick for me."

My dad liked to think he was friends with Dick. Sometimes I thought he envied the guy. I know he envied his bank account.

The security guard advanced, still blowing his whistle.

"I think he's serious," my dad said.

"I think you're right." I got out of the car. "Thanks for the ride."

I ended up next to the emergency exit, sitting next to a fat guy in a tan suit. A flight attendant with big hair showed us how to blow into the flotation devices even though we were flying over the desert.

Once we were airborne, the fat guy put his briefcase in his lap, popped it open and pulled out a *Penthouse*.

I tried to put my seat back, only to realize that it was broken. Maybe it wasn't broken—maybe it had something to do with being in an emergency row. But then why did they put the button on the arm rest? To taunt people?

So I sat bolt upright and watched the heavy engine dangle from the flimsy, flexing wing. And there was a cold draft leaking out of the bottom of the emergency door—I tried not to think about decompression.

After a while, I squeezed past the fat guy—he closed his briefcase and hugged it to his chest—and walked back to the bathroom. I shut the door behind me and slid the lock—the fluorescent light came on. It looked like someone had been popping zits onto the mirror and the sink was filled with soapy water.

Of course, just as I started pissing, the plane hit some turbulence and I pissed on my leg. When I flushed, my ears popped. I watched the blue stuff swirl down the stainless-steel toilet. There is something vaguely threatening about fluids on airplanes—it seems like anything could be airborne at any moment.

I didn't want to go back to my seat and the fat guy right away, so I hung out in the back and watched the stewardesses open and shut drawers. One of them turned around and caught me watching her.

She smiled. "You need anything, honey?"

"I'm okay," I said. "Thanks."

Dick picked me up at the Phoenix airport. He was wearing a white polo shirt and a big gold wristwatch on his muscular, orange arm.

He punched me in the shoulder. "Hey there, champ."

"Hi, Dick."

He smiled. He knew I enjoyed saying that.

"Your mom walked into the coffee table last night and banged up her knee pretty bad."

"She okay?"

"Yeah, but I don't think she'll be doing the tango any time soon."

"The tango," I said.

"It's a dance," Dick said. "What are you, stupid?"

"I know it's a dance. I'm just trying to picture my mom doing it."

"Your mom tangos very nicely. Don't be such a wise ass." He smiled and punched me in the arm again.

We walked out the sliding doors into the hot Arizona afternoon. Dick looked like he was lost for a second. Then he got his bearings.

"This way," he said.

Dick's dog, Ernie, was sitting in the front passenger seat of Dick's new BMW with his snout pressed up against the crack in the window. I knew that my mom didn't like being left home alone with the dog. Ernie wasn't fixed, so he was always trying to hump things. But Ernie pre-dated my mother—there wasn't much she could do.

Dick opened the door. "Get back there," he said. The dog jumped in back.

Dick cranked up the AC when he started the car, backed out of the space, then accelerated out of the parking lot. He really punched it getting onto the highway—my neck snapped back and Ernie clawed at the leather seats as he lurched backward.

"We've had some big rainstorms the last few days. Lots of lightning."

"Oh yeah?"

"You scared of lightning?"

"I guess."

"Hit my uncle when I was a kid. Killed him dead."

I said, "Geez."

He shrugged. "The guy was an asshole. That's when I started believing in God."

"You believe in God?"

"Nope," he said. "I stopped a week or two later when I fell off my bike and broke my arm." Then he said, "They feed you on the plane?"

"Peanuts."

"One bag or two?"

"One."

He shook his head. "That's hardly a decent lunch."

After a few miles, we got off the highway—Dick hit the exit ramp at about 80 mph, braking heavily. Almost immediately, he swerved into a Burger King drive-through.

"We don't have much food in the house. You want a cheeseburger or something?"

"No thanks."

"Sure? You'll be sorry later."

"Maybe a shake?"

He nodded. "The shakes are good. And I know your mom wants a fish sandwich."

We turned into the driveway and shot up the hill toward the house. There was another blast of hot air as we stepped out of the BMW. We walked across the bluish gravel walkway, then back into the cool AC of their house.

My mom was in bed with her leg up on a stack of pillows and a big ice pack strapped to her knee.

"Hi Mom." I leaned over and gave her a kiss.

My mom was looking very tan, and she had a fancy new dye job—blonde with reddish streaks. She was wearing a sweater. I loved that—a sweater in the cold house in the hot desert.

She shook her head. "I can't believe my timing."

"Does it hurt?"

"Not with all this ice."

"Don't get frostbite."

She took off the ice pack. The skin on her knee was blotchy—red and white. "How can you tell?" she said.

"I think your skin turns black."

Dick walked in, dropped the Burger King bag on the bed. "Brought you your fish sandwich."

My mom looked guilty. "My latest vice. I don't have them very often."

Dick laughed. "Bullshit."

So it was the reverse of my last visit—this time my mom was in bed, and I was bringing in the drinks and sandwiches. Somehow, that simplified things.

During the day, Dick left to play golf. My mom mostly watched TV and talked on the phone to her realtor buddies. I watched the big TV in the living room and wandered around the house—crossing back and forth across that small foot bridge. And sometimes, I went for short walks in the heat.

I liked the heat—liked the glare, liked the way the sun seemed to isolate you, a living creature making your way across the face of the Earth.

But generally, I felt kind of off the whole time I was there. Part of it had to do with being constipated—traveling always makes me constipated as hell. But basically, I felt useless. I usually feel useless, but it's easier to distract myself when I'm in my own environment. Here, though, I felt like an alien. A bored, useless, constipated alien.

We played cards at night. My mom insisted that we play at a table, so we helped her into the kitchen where she propped her leg up on a chair.

My mom is a Gin Rummy expert. I don't really understand the game. I get my ass kicked. But Dick kept the Scotch flowing, which took the edge off my humiliating losses. Ernie sat under the table and farted from time to time.

Since I had arrived, no one had said anything about Dick's son, Josh. Earlier in the day I'd come across a photo of him as a little kid—dressed up in a full cowboy outfit, pointing his cap gun at the family dog.

After a while, I said, "So where's Josh?"

Dick looked at my mom, then at me. "The little shit is in jail again."

"Again?"

"He's not in jail," my mom said. "Dick likes to exaggerate."

"Rehab, whatever. Same difference."

"He has a little problem with C-O-K-E," my mom said.

"Let's not talk about it," Dick said. He put down his card.

My mom smiled and lay down her cards. "Gin," she said.

"Jesus Christ," Dick said.

The next day I brought my mom a tuna sandwich and some cookies. I folded up a paper towel for her to use as a napkin—just like she used to do when we were kids.

My mom settled back against the pillow with the plate in her lap. "So we haven't had a real talk yet."

"Uh, no." I said. "I guess not."

"You can sit down. Here." She smoothed out the bedspread next to her.

I sat down.

She smiled. "So how are you?"

"Fine. How are you?"

She took a bite of her sandwich, and then with a full mouth said, "No, really."

"Great. I'm great." I flexed my bicep.

My mom laughed, wiped a bit of mayo off her lip. "Well, you always seem kind of down on the phone."

"That's the phone."

"You seem kind of down here, too."

"I do?"

"Yes. Maybe down isn't the word."

Here was the old "You seem depressed" comment I seemed to be getting a lot lately. It was like people wanted to make me feel guilty or something. I tried to look put out.

"I'm just concerned," she said. "That's all."

I shrugged. "I'm okay. Really."

She frowned. "Okay. I guess I'll have to take your word for it." She took another bite of her sandwich. Then she said, "How's your father?"

"Okay. Confused but okay."

"Is he getting along with Gwen?"

"I guess. I can't really tell."

"Your sister said he seemed antsy."

"He always seems antsy. That's his M.O."

"This is true." She looked across the room. "I still worry about him. I worry about both of you."

"You shouldn't. We're fine."

My mother sighed. I knew this sigh well—it was a sigh of frustration that had softened into more of a sigh of resignation over the years.

"Talk over?" I said.

"Yes," she said. "You're excused."

My last day there, I walked down to the edge of their property and watched their neighbor play tennis. She was wearing a short white dress and big Jackie O-style sunglasses and was practicing against a ball machine. The machine would shoot a tennis ball at her every few seconds. The entire court was littered with neon yellow tennis balls.

At one point she stepped back and tripped on one of the balls. Her ankle turned and then she went down like a sack of potatoes. I couldn't believe it. I started to run down there to see if she needed help, but there wouldn't be much I could do—she was fenced in. The ball machine kept shooting balls at her. After a moment, she stood up. She pulled at her dress a bit, then started hitting balls again.

I turned and walked back toward the house. I walked around the huge living and dining rooms that no one ever seemed to use, then around the side of my mom's bedroom. I stepped off the grass and onto the cedar chips and looked in the window.

My mom was on the bed, talking on the phone. She was laughing and doodling on a crossword puzzle she was holding in her lap.

My mom used to talk on the phone all the time when I was growing up. It drove me nuts. She'd talk and talk and talk, and I think it transported her out of our house. She always seemed so happy when she was on the phone— you could see it in her face, hear it in her voice. But after she got off the phone she'd kind of crash. She'd hang up and then she'd be back in our shitty house. I remember one time after a happy conversation with one of her friends, she hung up the phone and went and cried in her bedroom. I was maybe eight at the time and went to ask her what was wrong. She told me to leave her alone.

I'm sure that she was pretty miserable most of the time with my dad. But she always tried to play it cool, and she'd get really angry with us when we caught her being upset. The only other time she'd get angry with us was when we acted upset about something she thought was silly or selfish. She hated it when my sister and I bickered. Whenever I'd complain about something my sister had that I didn't, she'd snap, "Worry about yourself." She'd grown up in a big family—one of six kids—and I think this was something of a motto for her. My father, who was an only child, always acted pretty needy and whiny. I think my mother felt that people needed to be self-sufficient, and she looked down on people who weren't.

Now, looking through the window, I watched as she hung up the phone. Her face didn't fall the way it used to. She was still smiling as she went back to her crossword. Sometimes I thought she was a freak, but I have to admit, I was kind of proud of her. She was pretty tough.

Dick drove me back to the airport. I was wearing the windbreaker that my mom had tried to mail me earlier. It was dark blue, with "Nestron, Inc." embroidered on the front. It was actually kind of cool.

As soon as I got out Ernie jumped back in the front seat.

Dick said, "Come back anytime."

"Sounds good," I said.

"I know it sounds sappy, but your mom really likes seeing you."

"I like seeing her, too."

"I'm glad." Dick smiled. "Well, take care of yourself."

With that, he floored it, cutting off a taxi. I slung my bag over my shoulder and walked back into the airport.

Twenty

Inexplicably, and with little fanfare, my father and Gwen were back together. My father mentioned it in an off-hand manner when he called from the duplex. He couldn't find his electric razor and was wondering if he had left it at the house. I found it almost immediately—plugged into the bathroom electrical socket, recharging.

So Gordie and I had the house to ourselves again. The dumpster was gone and the house was pretty much empty. We had a new lawn and no kitchen. A realtor started bringing people by and giving tours. I'd be dozing on the couch and all of a sudden there'd be people looking at me. To my knowledge, no one had made an offer.

Meanwhile, the Barracuda needed a new alternator and a bunch of other stuff I didn't have money for. So it just sat in the driveway.

Gordie was in one of his mopey moods again. His job had gotten worse—one of the professors was using him as a glorified personal assistant, getting him to run errands, make phone calls, sort mail. And since his last trip to San Francisco, he had stopped hanging out with Jon no H. Plus, I think he was upset about Beth—neither of us had seen her since our trip to Santa Cruz, and I think he felt like he had humiliated himself.

One night, when we were at the Mexican place, Gordie started complaining about his job—saying that he wasn't so sure about this whole doctor thing anymore, that he didn't know why he was here, etc. I'd gotten another bloody nose in his truck on the drive over, dripping blood on the front of my shirt. So I was sitting there, listening to this and trying to eat a taco with a napkin wedged up my nose.

"Why don't you go home for a while?"

Gordie shook his head and said, "No way." I think he was trying to prove something to his family, to himself. Going home would mean admitting defeat.

But it obviously wasn't just homesickness or his job that was bugging him, because then he came out with a non-sequitur about Beth—something about her being "fickle." That's when I told him to relax, that he didn't have a chance with her anyway. That made him sit up.

"What do you mean?" he said.

"What do you mean, what do you mean?"

"I'm not..." He didn't finish.

"You're not what?"

He shook his head. "What about you?"

"What about me?"

Gordie and I just stared at each other for a moment. I suppose it wasn't any easier to lie to Gordie about my feelings for Beth than it was to lie to myself.

Gordie frowned slightly. Then he looked away.

Jack crashed hard in a race in Nevada City. He lost a lot of skin on the right side of his body—his leg, hip and arm were bandaged up and stiff as hell, but nothing was broken.

He was more upset about the Colnago—which he had raced for the first time. The brake levers were scuffed up, the wheels tweaked, and the frame got a nasty ding where the bars had swung around and whacked the top tube. The new paint was puckered up and starting to peel.

I was sitting on his bed, watching as he trued up his wheels and re-taped the bars. Sara, the foster kid, was splayed out on her stomach on the floor, scribbling in a Disney coloring book. Her dirty white socks waved back and forth in the air.

Jack started telling me about the crash: "The fucking idiot couldn't hold a line. I'd been watching him for a couple of laps, swinging wide of this manhole every time. Finally, he forced a guy into the curb—the guy went down, hit the hay bales, and then somehow bounced back into the rest of the field. Like twenty guys went down. I thought I was in the clear, but then I got taken down from behind."

The teacher had come to watch the race. She was horrified by the carnage—one guy got a chainring in his neck, another guy split his helmet open and was knocked out cold. She and Jack got into a big argument about it on the drive back home—she was saying that racing was much too dangerous, it shouldn't be legal, etc. Jack shook his head.

"I can't wait to get to Europe, man. People know how to ride bikes over there."

"You gonna bring Jill along?"

Jack smirked. "Right. She'd love it. They don't even wear helmets over there." He stood back, done with the tape job. "Look new again?"

"Better than new," I said. "Just broken in."

Sara jumped up, holding out the coloring book. "Look!"

We both looked. Minnie Mouse had red flames coming out of her eyes, green snot dripping from her nose.

Jack said, "Nice."

Gwen invited me and Gordie to dinner. She made a big deal out of it. She was going to cook her famous chicken casserole.

Gordie and I drove over in the truck. Just before we got there, Gordie made some sarcastic comment about Gwen—something about how he hoped she could cook better than she could paint (he had mentioned several times over the course of the summer how much he hated her painting of the Pantheon). Anyway, I knew it was hypocritical as hell, but I got defensive.

"Fuck you, man. You're living off my family and their hospitality and you're going to sit around and criticize them?"

Gordie said, "I'm sorry."

I felt kind of bad, but I was getting pretty tired of Gordie. And then I realized that I had referred to Gwen as "family"—I wasn't too sure how I felt about that.

We walked in and were hit with the stink of new carpet—my dad was convinced that he was being poisoned by the formaldehyde, and I could see why. But there were other smells, too. Kid smells. Bad cooking smells. And a nasty perfume smell.

The place was all white stucco, with hollow-sounding walls and cheesy brass doorknobs. My dad was sitting on the white leather couch with his shoes off, watching TV. He had been working a lot lately and had sold a few patents. None of it ever seemed to make him happy, though. Just more stressed.

Gwen was bustling around the kitchen in her Birkenstocks and oversized t-shirt. Gordie plopped himself down on one of the chrome stools and watched Gwen work.

Directly behind Gordie was a huge aquarium filled with goldfish. It took me a second to realize that they were my goldfish—adopted by Gwen when I left for Berkeley.

Sure enough there was the Godfather—a big black fish with a silly Dr. Seuss-style tail and bulging eyeballs. And there was Bubba, a bloated orange and white dude with what looked like a tumor on his stomach. About a week after I got him, he had turned over and floated to the top. At first I thought he was dead. But he was fine. He didn't seem to mind being upside-down and floating—in fact, he developed a pretty good backstroke. Plus, it gave him first shot at the food.

Gwen had replaced my old Goodwill tank with a fancy set-up—new pump, new filter. And she'd added a little treasure chest and Jules Verne-type scuba diver. The water was a hell of a lot cleaner—almost too clean if you ask me.

Gwen's kid Ben walked up to me while I was staring at the fish and started tugging on my arm. I grabbed a beer out of the fridge and let him drag me into his room.

I thought my room was a mess. His room was a disaster. First of all, that kid had a lot of toys. Toys in the closet, toys on shelves, toys all over the floor—and mostly all broken. Tonka trucks missing wheels, stuffed animals missing eyes, board games with their pieces scattered under the bed and dresser. And since his mom was an artist, she was trying to encourage Ben in the creative department. I don't know how much supervision there was, though. He'd gone nuts with the pens. There was pen all over the furniture, the bedspread, the walls—with a smattering of poster paint thrown in for good measure.

I was only just starting to notice that Ben was one of those kids who drooled a lot. He was kind of spitty. And the more excited he got, the more spit he generated. Soon his chin and neck were wet and shining.

We were playing a hybrid game with Legos and a large purple frog when my dad appeared at the door.

"What kind of pizza do you want?"

"What?" I said. "What happened to the casserole?"

"Burned."

Ben clapped and yelled, "Burned!"

"So what kind of pizza?"

"Pepperoni, I guess."

"Pepperoni!" Ben screamed.

"Pepperoni it is, then."

The pizza took forever to get there. Gwen disappeared into the bedroom for a while—I think to recover from a minor meltdown over the burned casserole—returning just in time to distract Ben, who was taking swigs from a two-liter bottle of Pepsi and working his way into a sugar-induced frenzy.

My dad and Gordie were talking about computers again. It was stupid but their little friendship was starting to bother me. And I don't know what bothered me more—Gordie's eagerness or my dad's enthusiasm over Gordie's interest.

The pizza finally came and we all ate while Gordie and my dad continued their conversation. Gwen looked sullen and Ben was getting tired and cranky. When he burst into a full-blown tantrum, Gordie and I got out of there.

We picked up *Caddyshack* on the way back and then dropped by Beth's place to see if she wanted to watch it with us. She was home with her mom and her mom's boyfriend—an old bald guy who had his new Harley Davidson parked out front—and glad to have the excuse to leave.

As we drove back to my house, Beth asked us what we would do if we won this lottery. This was one of her favorite questions. For her, it wasn't really a philosophical question. And the object wasn't to show how selfless you would be—in fact, she got angry once when I said I'd give it all to Mother Theresa. It had more to do with creativity.

I said what I usually said—that I'd put the money in the bank so I could live off the interest.

"Boring," Beth said.

"Alright," I said. "I'd spend it all on styrofoam. I'd buy up the world supply."

"Yeah, then what?"

"I don't know. I'd build a huge pyramid in the middle of the desert."

"Out of peanuts?"

"No, out of big blocks. Or maybe I'd build a really big igloo."

Beth laughed. "That's lame."

"Oh yeah? What would you do?"

Beth smiled. "I'd spend the money on more lottery tickets."

"I don't get it," I said.

"What do you mean? I'd buy ten million more lottery tickets."

"Oh," I said. "Great idea." Suddenly I felt tired. I wanted to take a nap.

Beth got really excited. "No, I know. I'd go to Vegas. Play roulette. Bet it all on lucky 13."

"They wouldn't let you," Gordie said.

"They'd let me."

"They wouldn't be able to cover a bet that large."

Beth was annoyed. "Alright Mr. Know-It-All, what would you do?"

Gordie shrugged. "I probably wouldn't play the lottery in the first place."

Beth shook her head. "No imagination."

The three of us were watching Bill Murray try to blow up the gopher when Pablo called.

"So check it out—Steve's parents have this huge house up near Mendocino. You gotta come up this weekend. We can hang out and party."

"With Mercedes Steve? No thanks."

"Dude, Chloe is gonna be there."

When I didn't say anything right away, Pablo said, "Come on, man. It'll be fun."

"My car died."

"So get Gordie to drive." He laughed. "I miss that guy."

"I'll think about it."

"Don't think too long."

When I hung up, Gordie said, "Who was that?"

"Pablo."

"How's Pablo?" Gordie said, as if he cared.

"Fine." I was weighing my options. Then I said, "You guys want to go up to Mendocino this weekend?"

Beth said, "I love Mendocino!"

Gordie said, "Is Pablo going to be there?"

"Yeah," I said. "He told me to invite you."

Gordie looked skeptical.

Beth said, "Let's go. It'll be fun."

Twenty-one

We took Beth's Subaru. We loaded Gordie up on Dramamine and put him in the front seat. It was a station wagon, so I put the back seat down, made myself a bed and tried to sleep. Beth's driving scared the shit out of me. I couldn't watch.

We headed up through the city—identical pastel-colored houses lining Nineteenth Avenue—and then across the Golden Gate Bridge, its big red towers cartoonish against the blue sky. Then up Highway 101 through Marin County, through Santa Rosa, heading north.

It seemed to grow hotter after we left the freeway and turned west, toward the ocean. There were warnings posted alongside the road: FIRE DANGER: HIGH. The dead grass was almost white in the sun.

Pretty soon we were on narrow, winding roads. Beth and I switched places, and then I was working that little Subaru hard, downshifting to second to get over steep grades. Rows of vineyards passed by like flip books.

I kept going back and forth about Chloe. I don't know what my problem was. She was good looking, funny, smart—not that that actually meant anything—plenty of good looking, smart, funny psychos out there. But I always over-analyzed stuff. I'd ask Pablo what he thought of some girl and it was like a yes/no question for him. I got all hung up in the gray areas—gray areas that I'd invent before I even knew the person. I'd look for faults just to have an excuse. It was stupid. It was fear.

The house sat right up on a bluff overlooking the ocean. After all that still heat, here was wind, here was haze and fog and mist. I put on my new windbreaker after we got out of the car.

As it turned out, Mercedes Steve, Pablo and Anne were in town buying provisions. So when we walked in, it was just Chloe and this kid I had only heard about—Jake, the teenage step-brother, problem child and petty arsonist. I looked at him with his backwards baseball cap and earring and thought about those fire warnings.

Chloe gave me a hug, then stood back and looked at my windbreaker. "What's Nestron, Inc.?"

"Huge multinational. They make everything from breakfast cereal to waterbeds."

Chloe raised her eyebrows. "Wow." She looked good—tan and kind of wind-blown.

I introduced Beth and the drugged-out Gordie and then Chloe showed us into the house—low ceilings, the main room dark in the late afternoon, with big windows looking out at the dull gray ocean.

Chloe said, "The boys are downstairs. Beth, we're sharing a room upstairs."

Chloe took Beth upstairs and Gordie collapsed on the couch.

Jake was just kind of staring at me with his hands in his pockets.

"How's it going?" I said.

He shrugged. Then he said, "You got any pot?"

"No," I said. "Sorry."

Beth and Chloe came back downstairs, laughing and talking like they were already best friends. The three of us left Gordie—asleep again—and went out to the beach, followed by the sullen Jake.

We walked through the tall grass then down steep, sandy dunes to the beach. The waves made green foam on the dark, hard sand.

Beth took in a deep breath and said, "I love the air here."

Chloe said, "It's great, isn't it?"

Beth said, "Do you come out here every summer?"

"Pretty much."

"Must be nice," Beth said. Then she gave me a look.

Chloe caught the look, but didn't seem to mind. She said, "Nice in a boring kind of way."

I looked out to sea. A big oil tanker was on the horizon. Farther down the beach, Jake was throwing rocks at seagulls.

"Hey," I said. "That's not cool."

Chloe laughed.

Jake looked at me, then threw another rock.

Beth picked up a stick and threw it at Jake. He had to dodge it.

"Nice throw," I said.

Beth smiled. "Thanks."

We got back to the house just as Mercedes Steve and Pablo were lugging in a case of gin. Pablo was wearing baggy Bermuda shorts and a big straw hat.

"Isn't that a bit excessive?" Chloe said.

"It was on sale," Mercedes Steve said. Then he said, "Colin, could you move your car? That's where I park my car."

This type of bullshit drove me nuts, but I didn't want to get off to a bad start. I turned to Beth. "Want to move it?"

Beth raised her eyebrows slightly.

"I'll move it," Jake said.

I laughed. "You have a driver's license?"

"Learner's permit."

Mercedes Steve said, "He's good at it."

Beth looked to me for some kind of sign. Then she shrugged and handed over her keys.

Pablo said, "I like the jacket. What's Nestron?"

"Defense contractor. They make fuel-air explosives and toilet seats."

"Cool."

Anne came in with a bag of groceries. "Hi guys!"

More hugs. I saw then that Beth and Pablo were eyeing each other. I realized that they had never met. I introduced them.

Pablo said, "Yeah, I heard about you."

Beth laughed and looked pleased.

There were horrible revving sounds coming from outside.

"What is he doing to my car?" Beth said.

Pablo smiled. "I'm glad that's not my car."

Gordie walked into the kitchen looking hungover. "What time is it?"

"Time for you to wake up, buddy!" Pablo said.

Gordie yawned. He was too tired to do battle with Pablo.

We were making dinner—a big pot of spaghetti. Chloe chopped vegetables while I stirred onions around in a frying pan. Anne sliced up garlic bread and Mercedes Steve mixed gin and tonics for everyone.

Chloe dumped a bunch of chopped carrots in the pot while I was stirring.

"You're messing up my program here," I said.

Chloe laughed. "Your program?"

"I have a system, you know."

"Which is it?"

"Which is what?"

"Is it a system or a program?"

"The program is incorporated into the system. And the system is part of a larger culinary scheme."

"Oh," she said. "Do you want me to take the carrots out?"

"It's too late for that now."

She smiled. "Good."

This overt bit of flirtation was somewhat embarrassing. But Pablo was worse—I heard him telling Beth how much he loved Paris, and I was pretty sure he'd never been there.

I asked Pablo, "Where's Clarissa?"

Pablo looked irritated. "Ummmm, not here?"

Anne said, "Pablo is acting like a baby."

"I'm acting like a baby?"

"What happened?" I said.

"We broke up."

"You did not," Anne said.

"Yeah we did."

"Don't listen to him," Anne said.

Pablo just shook his head.

At dinner, Mercedes Steve said, "The onions weren't cooked enough."

I looked at Chloe. "See," I said.

"Oh shut up," Chloe said.

"They're perfect," Anne said. "It tastes great."

Jake was pulling out bits of zucchini and putting them on the side of his plate.

Pablo raised his gin and tonic. "A toast."

"To what?" Beth said.

"To Gordie," Pablo said. "For wearing that shirt."

We all stared at Gordie and his fairly innocuous polo shit.

"What's wrong with this shirt?" Gordie said.

"Nothing," Pablo said. "I like it, that's why I'm toasting it."

"Whatever," Gordie said. He glanced at Beth.

"To Gordie's shirt," Beth said, smiling at Pablo.

Everyone clinked glasses.

After dinner, Chloe and I ended up sitting outside on the back porch—on a wood bench with mildewed cushions. The sun had gone down without me noticing. Moonlight played across the phosphorescent surf.

"You been having a good summer?" I said.

"Okay. You?"

"Yeah, great."

There was a silence. When it got down to it, I wasn't a very good talker.

Then Chloe said, "Pablo said you were kind of depressed or something."

"Depressed?" Fucking Pablo. I was going to have to get him back for this. "Depressed about what?"

Chloe shrugged. "I don't know."

"About the fate of mankind?"

"The fate of mankind?"

"I don't know," I said. "I just said that to be funny."

"Well, it was funny."

"Thanks."

Chloe smiled but didn't say anything.

I was suddenly very aware of being nineteen. I wished I was older. I wasn't much better than that kid, Jake.

So we just sat there for a while, just looking out at the stupid water. Then, abruptly, she kissed me. We started kissing a bit, then I felt it—another nosebleed. I sat back, fast, putting my hand to my face.

"Fuck."

"What?"

I stood up. "I'll be right back."

I ran into the house, into the bathroom, swearing to myself. "Shit, shit, shit, shit."

I looked in the mirror. Slowly, I pulled my hand away, waiting for the geyser. Nothing. It had already stopped.

I washed up and went back outside. Chloe stood up.

"I think I'm going to go upstairs."

"Upstairs?" I said.

"Yeah, I'm pretty tired." She smiled. "Goodnight." She walked inside.

I just stood there, pissed. I felt like an idiot. Then I saw that fucking kid—Jake. He had been sitting over in the far corner the whole time, watching.

"What are you looking at?" I said.

"Nothing."

"Good answer," I said. I got up and walked inside.

Pablo and Gordie and Beth were sitting on the couch, watching TV. Beth was sandwiched between Pablo and Gordie. It made me feel vaguely ill.

So I was stuck—the main room was supposed to be my bedroom. I walked out front.

Beth's Subaru was in a ditch, with the parking lights on and the windshield wipers stuck at the top of their sweep. That kid had done a great job.

I turned and looked at the house. I could see a light upstairs. It was only ten o'clock.

I went and turned off Beth's parking lights. Then I walked back inside to look for the gin.

Twenty-two

The next morning people started crashing around early. Pablo and I had gotten into an impromptu gin drinking competition after Beth and Gordie went to bed, and when I woke up, it felt like someone was trying to drive a diamond through my forehead.

I was trying to ignore people, trying to get back to sleep when Beth started tugging at my arm, telling me I should get up and go on a horseback ride with them. I mumbled something about animal abuse and she left me alone. Soon they were gone and the house was quiet again.

Pablo and I were lying on opposite couches, staring blankly at the ceiling. The headache had moved behind my left eye and had diminished somewhat.

After a while, Pablo said, "Beth is pretty cool."

"Gordie thinks so, too"

Pablo laughed. "Fucking Gordie, man." Then he said, "So what's up with you and Chloe? You gonna fuck her or what?"

"Uh," I said. "Sure?"

"Seriously."

"What?"

"Seriously. Are you gonna fuck her?"

"Man, shut up."

Pablo sat up. "Don't tell me you're still being a fucking monk."

"No."

"That's good. You were starting to worry me there for a second." Pablo lay back. "Then there's Gordie—what's up with that guy, anyway?"

"I don't know," I said. "He's been pretty grumpy lately."

"Fucking Grinch who stole Christmas. And the guy won't take a hint. I was getting ready to punch him last night."

I wanted to change the topic, so I said, "So what's up with that kid Jake?"

Pablo laughed. "I love Jake. He's a trip."

"That kid gets on my nerves."

"Where is he, anyway?" Pablo sat up again and yelled, "Hey Jake!" Jake!"

"He's hiding," I said.

"Come out you little shit!" Pablo yelled. "Come make us some breakfast!"

It was almost two o'clock by the time we got up. We cooked some eggs and the gourmet chicken sausages Mercedes Steve had bought in Mendocino. Afterwards, we went to sit out on the back porch. That's when we discovered the croquet set.

The mallets were grass-stained and chipped and the gates were bent and rusted, but it was complete. Pablo and I went out back and set up a challenging course, with obstacles and sand traps.

We were practicing when everyone returned from the horseback ride. Gordie was limping—inevitably, he had ended up with the oldest, most senile horse. The animal had tried to rub him off on a tree.

"That's what you get," I said.

Anne smiled when she saw the croquet set. "Croquet? Are we going to play croquet?"

"Hell yes," Pablo said.

"Uh oh," she said. "I know how you guys play."

"What do you mean?" Pablo said.

"Play nice," Chloe said. She was wearing tight riding pants.

Gordie had stopped to examine one of the mallets.

"You gonna play Gordie?" Pablo said.

He shrugged. "I guess."

"Good," Pablo said. "I'm gonna kick your ass."

"I have to change," Chloe said.

"Me, too," said Beth.

"Go change," Pablo said. "We'll be here."

When it comes to croquet, there are two schools of thought. One is to play the game more or less like one would play golf—that is, take turns, be polite, try to get through the course quickly and elegantly. The other approach is to treat the game like a smash-up derby. Here, the best defense is a good offense, and the goal is not necessarily to win, but to drive other people's balls as far off the course as possible—to sabotage serious play and humiliate your opponent.

So it was like two separate games. Beth and Anne and Chloe leapt out front while Pablo and I lagged behind, trying to knock each other out of the game. Gordie wasn't too far ahead—he was having trouble getting through one of the gates.

Of course, Pablo made a special effort where Gordie was concerned. When Pablo sent Gordie's ball flying into the sand trap, Gordie said, "You guys are dicks."

Pablo and I were still in the middle of the course when the three girls turned and started making their way back to the finish. Beth was in the lead and I was in a position to knock her ball. She said, "Colin, don't even think about it."

"Get her," Pablo said.

Beth turned sternly to Pablo. "You shut your mouth."

I tried for Beth's ball and missed.

"Oh come on," Pablo said. "You missed on purpose."

"No," Beth said. "Colin is just a nice person."

"I don't know about that," Pablo said.

I think Beth had already won when Pablo knocked Gordie's ball into some prickly bushes. We all had to help him find it. Finally, Chloe spotted it. You could only see it from one angle. It was deep in there.

Gordie said, "Go get it, Pablo."

"Hey, buddy, that's your ball. You get it."

Mercedes Steve had steered clear of the game in order to set up the barbecue on the beach. With Jake's help, he had gotten the grill going. Smoke was wafting toward us.

"Cookout time," Pablo said.

"We're not done yet," Gordie said, emerging with the ball, his shirt covered with sticky thorns. "We have some unfinished business."

Pablo shrugged. "I'm done." He headed toward the beach.

Gordie shook his head in disbelief. "Fucking asshole."

We started drinking again—the only true cure for a hangover. Mercedes Steve lumped all sorts of meat onto the grill. He was wearing an apron and taking orders.

We ate, we drank. Soon it was dark.

After dinner, we gathered driftwood for a fire. Pablo and I dragged a large tree trunk over. Jake doused the pile with an entire can of lighter fluid and tossed in a match. Huge flames leapt into the sky.

We all sat around the fire. Gordie and Mercedes Steve started talking about medical school. I was sitting next to Chloe. Her face was lit up by the fire's orange glow.

All of a sudden, Chloe jumped. "Ouch!"

"What?" I said.

"A spark." She looked at her sock. "Look, a hole."

Sure enough, there was a small burn hole in her white sock.

"My sock melted." Then she said, "I thought these socks were cotton."

"Fifty fifty," Beth said. She was huddled up to Pablo.

Chloe rubbed her ankle. "I'm taking them back."

Jake appeared with an old tire. Before anyone could stop him, he tossed it onto the flames.

"Nice one," Pablo said.

Black smoke started billowing out of the fire. When I got up to move out of the way, Chloe took my hand. She pulled me away. We started walking down the beach.

When we were far from the fire, she looked at me and smiled. We stopped and kissed.

We started walking again, and then, when I wasn't looking, she picked up a huge piece of kelp and shoved it down the back of my shirt.

By the time I managed to get the kelp out of my shirt, she was already running. She ran down along the water and then swept up along the dunes. I was about to catch her when all of a sudden I was flying head over heels. I landed on my ass, hard.

Chloe walked up to me, laughing. "You okay?"

I wasn't sure. The breath had been knocked out of me.

"Oh shit," Chloe said, laughing and almost falling backwards.

"What?" I said. That's when I noticed the smell. I looked around and saw it—I'd tripped over a dead sea lion. It was bloated and stinking. I had sea lion guts on me. I got up in a hurry.

"Don't touch me," she said, backing away and laughing. "Don't touch me."

She ran away again. I chased her a bit, but then I slowed down. My back was killing me.

I caught back up with Chloe at the bonfire. The tire had burned itself out and the fire was pretty much just coals. Anne was leaning against Steve, and Gordie was sitting there looking sullen. Beth and Pablo were conspicuously absent.

"Stay away," Chloe said, still laughing.

I smelled my arm. It smelled like dead sea lion.

"I'm gonna go wash up," I said. I headed back toward the house. All of a sudden, Gordie appeared right next to me.

"Are we friends?" he said.

"What?" I said.

"Are we friends?"

"Yeah," I said. "Why?"

Gordie didn't answer.

When we walked into the dark house, Gordie flipped on the light. Pablo and Beth were on the couch. Pablo said, "Turn off the light."

Looking back on this, I would say that Gordie wanted me there to share his humiliation. I think he also held me responsible in some way.

Pablo and Beth were sitting up now. Beth cleared her throat and attempted to straighten out her hair.

Pablo said, "Can we... help you?"

Gordie was staring at Beth. His face was bright red. After a moment, he turned and walked out of the room. We heard the kitchen door slam.

Pablo shook his head. "That guy. I swear." When his eyes met mine, a smile slowly spread across his face.

I turned and went upstairs.

I took my time in the shower. I cranked up the hot water until the whole bathroom was filled with steam.

To say I felt nothing when I saw Pablo with Beth would be a lie, but I had been distracted by the whole thing with Chloe, by the dead sea lion, by Gordie. When Gordie switched on the light, I felt disoriented, disconnected—

almost invisible. It was Pablo's smug smile that snapped me out of my little trance—and then all I felt was shame.

Now, as I scrubbed away at the sea lion guts, the shame melted into something that more closely resembled anger. Fuck Beth and Pablo. Fuck Chloe. Fuck Gordie. Fuck all of them. I didn't care.

When I got back downstairs, Pablo said, "Gordie took Steve's car."

"What?" I said.

"He drove off. He's gone."

"How did he get the keys?"

"Fucking Jake. He moved Steve's car and I guess he left the keys on the kitchen counter."

"The valet extraordinaire," Beth said. She was wearing Pablo's sweatshirt.

"Does Steve know?"

"No," Pablo said. "And I think I'm gonna let you tell him."

"Let's wait and see if he comes back."

Beth looked at Pablo. Then she said, "I'm not sure he's coming back."

"Why?"

"He took his stuff."

I looked around and saw that it was true. Gordie's backpack was gone.

"Great," I said. "That's great."

Mercedes Steve didn't take it too well. He started pacing back and forth and taking deep breaths. "I'm gonna call the cops," he said.

"Now just calm down," Anne said.

Mercedes Steve said, "Asshole." He seemed to be looking for something to break. He picked up a small ceramic bowl off the mantelpiece, but then thought better of it and put it back.

"Look. What is he going to do?" Anne said. "He's not going to do anything."

"He better not, that's all I can say," Mercedes Steve said.

I was sitting on the couch. I had scrubbed pretty hard in the shower, but I could still smell the dead sea lion.

"Jesus," Mercedes Steve said. "Jesus H Fucking Christ."

"He'll come back," I said.

"Oh yeah? How do you know?"

"Cause I know Gordie."

"He seems like a real freak if you ask me." Mercedes Steve looked right at me when he said this—like it was an accusation.

"You're the freak," I said.

"What?"

"You heard me."

"Let's all calm down," Anne said.

"No," Mercedes Steve said. "No." He was practically sputtering.

Pablo was looking at me, smirking. I could tell he was enjoying this. Chloe was staring down at the carpet.

Mercedes Steve walked out of the room and slammed the door. After a moment, Anne followed.

"Nice going, dude," Pablo said. He patted me on the back.

"Fuck you, Pablo."

"Oh!" Pablo said. "Colin is pissed!"

I just shook my head. I couldn't really look at Pablo. If I did, I thought I might laugh, which didn't seem like such a good idea. Still, the whole thing was pretty funny. And I was vaguely impressed, too—I felt kind of proud of Gordie.

So we all just sat around, not talking. Pablo turned on the TV but nobody watched. At one point, I caught Chloe's eye, but she looked away. I couldn't figure out what that was supposed to mean.

Then the phone rang.

Beth and I drove to the hospital. It was down in Bodega Bay, where Hitchcock had filmed "The Birds."

Apparently, Gordie had headed down Highway One at high speed. He lost it on a corner and slid into a tree. The Mercedes was totaled. Gordie wasn't in great shape himself. They had to bring in the jaws of life.

I hate hospitals. I hate the way they smell, I hate those long linoleum hallways, and I hate all the empty wheelchairs, stacked up in rows like grocery carts. And then there's those weird shoes that nurses wear—those off-white leather shoes with the big rubber soles. I couldn't help staring at them as Beth and I followed the nurse back to Gordie's room.

When we walked in, Gordie didn't want to look at Beth. Beth walked out and then it was just me and Gordie.

I said, "So I guess your Formula One career is over."

Gordie didn't say anything. His face was all swollen and lumpy. They were worried about internal bleeding.

There was a bunch of ancient-looking hospital equipment in the room—stuff right out of an old Frankenstein movie. And everything was painted beige.

"Hey, at least you'll get a life supply of pain medication. That ought to be worth something."

Gordie still didn't smile. I don't know—maybe it hurt to smile.

I shrugged. I didn't really know what to say. I certainly wasn't going to apologize—I mean, I felt sorry for him, but the whole thing was his own damn fault.

Then Gordie said, "Stupid."

"What?" I said.

He shook his head. "Everyone."

After that, Beth and I drove home. Gordie's parents were going to fly in and take care of him.

The ride home was quiet. I let Beth drive. I was sure she'd steer us into a big rig any moment, but I was too tired to care.

Beth said, "I feel like it's my fault."

"It is."

"Do you mean that?"

"No."

The truth of the matter is, I was feeling sorry for myself. I was thinking about Chloe. I had barely talked to her after we found out about Gordie. I thought she had acted kind of funny. But then, I guess her loyalties were divided.

Beth said, "You think he'll be okay?"

"Sure," I said. "He'll be fine."

Twenty-three

I pulled the first bike out of the box, unwrapped the frame and put it in the work stand. Then I went through the routine: I trued up the wheels, checked the fixed cup, adjusted the bottom bracket, tightened down the lock nut on the headset. I greased the stem, inserted the handlebar assembly and put on the front wheel. Then I turned back to the work bench to unwrap the rest of the stuff—pedals, reflectors, brake housing, the seat and seat post.

It was only nine o'clock. I hadn't been up that early all summer. But Jack's shop had just received its shipment of fall bikes, and I was their fall bike guy. For the past few summers, I had been coming in around this time of year, building bikes at ten bucks a pop. Fifty bikes and I'd have enough money to get the Barracuda back on the road.

There were three repair stands. I was at the back, closest to the window. The wood bench was pockmarked from years of use. The tools hung on the walls in rows, with each set color coded by the bench. My tools were the worst set by far, incomplete and badly worn.

Jeff, the head mechanic, always made a big pot of coffee when he came in, so I had my coffee on the bench along with a bagel from the deli next door. I kept wiping cream cheese and grease on my apron.

Jeff was building a wheel—he had just finished lacing it up, and was starting the slow, careful process of tensioning. Jeff was a big guy, in his mid-thirties, and had been working in shops forever. I had learned not to talk to him or to play the radio before he'd had his coffee.

Just as I was finishing the first bike, Jack rode in, late. He unclipped from his bike and went to hang it up in back. He emerged from the bathroom a minute later wearing cut-offs and an apron and the high tops he kept at the shop. He punched in, then pulled the first repair ticket of the morning—for an old Schwinn which he retrieved from the back and clamped into the stand.

He frowned, then backed away from the bike.

"The fuck?"

"What?" I said.

"There's dog shit on the tires."

"That's why I like new bikes," I said.

Jack popped the bike out of the stand and unceremoniously shoved it toward the back area. It bounced off the small parts drawers and crashed into a pile of rims.

Jeff was putting the finishing touches on the wheel. He looked up at the noise.

"No violence," Jeff said.

Jack disappeared and then came back with a new-looking mountain bike.

After a few bikes, I went out back for a break.

The repair area opened onto a fenced-in courtyard. Jeff kept the parts washer out there because of the fumes. There were a few potted plants and a mess of rusty bike parts piled in the corner—wheels with the hubs cut out, broken frames, handlebars and forks.

I sat in one of the mildewed vinyl chairs. It was nice out there, with the sun fading in and out as clouds passed overhead. Smells from the Chinese restaurant next door wafted across the courtyard, mingling with the odor of oil and solvent.

It had been two weeks since the whole thing in Mendocino. I had called Gordie several times—had left messages with his parents—but I hadn't heard back. I knew that he was okay—his parents had told me that much. But I got the feeling that Gordie was angry, that he was avoiding me.

Jeff came out for his mid-morning smoke. This was a sign that we were getting into the verbal part of the day. Soon the radio would be on.

He sat next to me and lit up. He dropped a few ashes into a rusted coffee can that had been put there for that purpose.

"I checked over one of your bikes," he said.

"Oh yeah? How was it?"

"You still suck at wheels."

"I know," I said. "But I'm cheap."

He laughed. "That's true." Then he said, "Jack okay?"

"I think so."

"He seems kind of angry or something."

I shrugged. But I had noticed the same thing. Normally Jack was in a good mood and fairly talkative after his rides. But this morning he had been quiet. And it wasn't just the dog shit.

Jack walked out. "Hey Jeff, your favorite customer is here."

"The girl who doesn't wear any panties?"

"No, the old guy with the Bendix hub. He says you sold him the wrong part."

Jeff swore and put out his cigarette. He walked back into the shop mumbling.

Jack sat down. He spit between his feet. Then he said, "She dumped my ass."

"What?"

"She went back to that lawyer guy."

It took me a second to figure out what he was talking about—the teacher, Jill.

"That sucks," I said.

Jack shrugged, then spit again—this time it dangled there a second.

I knew he wouldn't say anything more. If it had been Pablo, he would have launched into a long diatribe. But that wasn't Jack's style. It was funny, though—I think it was the first time someone had dumped Jack, not the other way around.

Just then, Sam, the owner, came out the back door. "You boys gonna jump on the dumpster for me?"

Jack stood up. "Hell yes."

The shop produced a surprising amount of garbage—more than would fit easily into a standard dumpster. But the old man was too cheap to pay for two. So dumpster jumping was part of the routine.

Jack got really into it, jumping up and down like it was a trampoline. I was more tentative—I held onto the side with one hand.

We were jumping on all sorts of stuff—cardboard, old wheels, plastic packaging and burned-out fluorescent light bulbs. Then abruptly, Jack stopped.

"Oh shit," he said.

"What?"

Jack had sunk down a bit on one side. Slowly, he pulled his leg up. His shoe and sock were soaked with wet, black grease. Jack reached down and pulled out a big vat of cooking oil.

Jack looked more disappointed than angry. "I told those guys," he said.

He jumped down out of the dumpster. Then, holding the vat of grease out in front of him, he walked through the back door of the Chinese restaurant.

I heard some yelling, followed by a crash. A few seconds later, Jack came back out, grinning.

"What did you do?" I said.

"I gave it back."

When Gordie called finally, I didn't recognize his voice.

"Who is this?" I said.

"It's Gordie," he said.

It was late afternoon. I had just come back from the shop and was cooking some ramen noodles—one of my specialties. I liked to stir in the MSG packet, then drain off all the liquid and eat it like spaghetti.

"How are you doing?" I said.

"I'm sending someone for the truck," he said, flatly.

"What?" I said. "Why?"

There was a pause. "I'm not coming back."

"You're not?"

"I'm going to transfer to Ohio State."

I said, "Oh." His father was finally getting his way.

"The guy should be there by Thursday morning."

"Thursday," I said. "Got it."

"Well, nice knowing you."

"Yeah," I said. I was trying to think of something to say—something other than, "Nice knowing you, too."

Gordie said, "Have a nice life." And then he hung up.

Beth said, "Have a nice life?"

I had gone over to Beth's work—to the Gift Shoppe—right after Gordie's call. I wasn't sure whether to be amused or offended.

Beth was gift-wrapping a box of nasty-looking orange chocolates for this old lady with a bald spot. Beth smiled and shook her head. "That's lame."

"That's Gordie," I said.

"You think he's mad at us or something?"

"I wouldn't be surprised."

"What a baby."

Beth finished tying a gold ribbon and handed the box to the old lady, who seemed pleased. We watched as she waddled away.

Then Beth perked up. "Pablo called me."

"He's a suave guy."

"He is!" She laughed.

Another old lady—this one wearing a magenta jumpsuit—walked up holding a porcelain bear. "Do you have any more of these? This one is damaged."

The bear had an obvious chip on one of its ears. Beth said, "It's supposed to be like that."

The lady said, "It's supposed to be chipped?"

Beth shrugged, somehow managing to keep a straight face. The old lady walked off, miffed.

Then Beth said, "Have you called Chloe?"

"No."

"You should call her."

I smiled. I could hear the magenta lady complaining to one of Beth's co-workers.

Beth said, "Seriously. You should call her."

"I'll think about it," I said. In fact, Chloe had been in my mind quite a bit lately. Sometimes, I liked to think that events had conspired against me, but that was a convenient excuse.

Beth smiled. "You're just a hopeless romantic, aren't you?"

When I got back to the house I went and sat in Gordie's truck. Gordie had never gotten the damage fixed—his insurance had a high deductible, and he would have had to cover the cost of the repairs. So it still looked like it did the day we left Berkeley—bits of glass on the floor and wires hanging out of the dash. And after many nights of sitting outside with the busted window, it was starting to smell a bit moldy.

From the first day at Berkeley, I had treated Gordie as something of an experiment. We had almost nothing in common (though I'm not sure what that means—is that interest or simply a matter of temperament?). But I had tried to withhold judgment and had viewed him as something of a curiosity.

The question is: Why had I chosen to EXTEND this little experiment? I could have easily told him to go fuck himself at the end the year. I certainly didn't owe him anything (though I felt vaguely sorry for him—which is somewhat ridiculous, and I was irritated by that impulse in myself). In any case, I knew he would probably be a pain in the ass and that I would regret it—but for some reason, that didn't really bother me, either.

Basically, I think I had been afraid of the empty house— afraid that returning home was some kind of failure. So I welcomed having someone around to break up the monotony, to provide some distraction. But I hadn't anticipated all the weirdness with Beth, nor his friendship with my father. Both of these things had bothered me—and the fact that they had bothered me bothered me even more.

To be honest, I was glad that he was gone. But now something was different—I felt like I had entered some kind of purgatory. Gordie had served as a reminder that I had a life outside this place—that I had some kind of future. Now I wasn't so sure.

Just then, Mrs. Patrick pulled into her driveway. She got out and opened the trunk, revealing a mass of grocery bags. I climbed out of Gordie's truck and jogged across the street to help.

Twenty-four

I built bikes like a maniac—five or six per day. Pretty soon the whole showroom was filled with my handiwork—a bunch of shitty Taiwanese mountain bikes. Red or blue, your choice.

One afternoon I got home from bike building to find my father sitting in the middle of the new front lawn with a bottle of scotch. He didn't drink, so I knew something was up.

"Sold," he said.

"The house?"

"The house. It's sold." He took a slug of scotch.

I sat down next to him. "I guess the new lawn did the trick, huh?"

My dad shook his head. "The guy's gonna bulldoze it, start over."

"Smart man."

My dad shrugged. "Seems like a waste if you ask me."

My dad had seemed pretty out of it lately. I don't think he had even noticed that Gordie was gone.

"Where did you get the scotch?" I said.

He looked at the bottle like he had forgotten about it. Then he said, "Remember Infotek, that company I worked for when we first moved here?"

"I guess," I said. I didn't.

"They gave these out at the Christmas party. I found it in the back of my closet."

"That's some old scotch."

"Tastes like paint thinner. Want some?"

"No thanks," I said.

My dad shook his head. "So it's done. It's a done deal."

"If the guy doesn't want it, maybe we can keep the lawn," I said. "You know, roll it back up and take it with us?"

He nodded—he actually seemed to consider it. "Not a bad idea," he said. "Not a bad idea."

It wasn't completely a done deal. There was plenty of paperwork. But soon, I was going to be out of a place to live.

The Patricks offered to let me stay with them for the rest of the summer. My father offered the same thing—to stay with him and Gwen—but that didn't seem like a good idea to me.

The guy came to pick up Gordie's truck bright and early—right in the middle of my breakfast. He was skinny, in his mid-twenties, with a little mustache—it looked like it had taken him about three years to grow it. He had his buddy waiting out front in an old Ranchero.

He looked pretty bummed when he saw the truck. I didn't blame him. If you signed up for a drive away, you probably imagined yourself having some kind of Jack Kerouac experience in a big Cadillac, not some crappy pickup.

"The window's busted?"

"Yup," I said.

"No stereo?"

"Guess not."

He looked at Gordie's stuff, which I had loaded in the bed. "What's with all the crap in the back?"

"You're asking the wrong guy."

The guy just shook his head. He glanced back at his friend, then said, "Can I use your phone?"

"Sure."

I showed him inside. He looked around the house—at all the emptiness and disrepair. Jack and I had gotten drunk the night before and started fucking around with a lighter and a can of WD-40. There were burn marks on the walls and ceiling.

"Damn. What happened in here?"

I shrugged. "Same thing that happened to the truck."

The guy frowned.

I pointed out the phone, then went back to my cereal. When he was done with his call, he said, "Alright."

"Okay," I said.

He walked outside. A minute later, I heard the truck start and drive away. My Gordie souvenir sat in front of me on the coffee table. It was tall and gold and shiny. Gordie, the debate team champion.

I was making a final pass through the house when I decided I better call my sister about her stuffed animals. I was pretty sure that she would want some of them for the kids—at least Squirrel.

I called her up. Hubby answered.

"Colin!" He had a booming voice. You could hear it echo off the walls of the room. "How are things? You having a good summer?"

"Great summer," I said.

"Glad to hear it!"

"My sister there?"

"She is! Can you hold on a second?"

I guess it wasn't really a question, because before I could answer, the phone slammed down on the table. I heard him yelling for her, heard the TV in the background.

My sister came to the phone a minute later.

"Colin, I'm so glad you called."

I waited for a reason she was glad—for some big announcement. But there was none. So I asked her about the stuffed animals.

She laughed. "That's so funny."

"You want me to send them to you?"

"Oh no, don't worry about it. They'd probably give the kids a rash or something."

"So what should I do?"

"I don't know. Give them away, throw them out, whatever you want."

"Even Squirrel?"

She laughed. "Poor Squirrel. Yes, even Squirrel."

It was stupid, but I couldn't help feeling disappointed. I guess this is how my mom had felt about that stupid windbreaker. It also kind of emphasized how much my sister had moved on. I was still bogged down in the house, in all this useless crap.

Then she said, "So, still having a good summer?"

"Great summer," I said.

A few nights later, Beth called. "Colin, can you come over here?"

"Why?" I was watching TV in the nearly empty living room.

"Just get over here, okay?"

"Yes, ma'am."

The Plymouth was still dead so I had to walk.

Beth's mom answered the door wearing a Harrah's Reno t-shirt. I always felt embarrassed around Beth's mom. She seemed kind of nutty. I also could never tell what she thought of me—she always looked at me slightly sideways and seemed to be smirking.

She said, "Hi Colin. They're in the living room."

Dan was passed out on the couch.

"He fell asleep," Beth said.

"I can see that. Why'd you let him in?"

"My mom did. But now she doesn't want him on the couch. She thinks he'll puke or something."

"We could put plastic under him."

"No, I want to put him back in his car. That way, when he wakes up, he can just drive away."

"An excellent plan."

Beth giggled. "Come on."

We each grabbed him under an armpit and dragged. He was heavy.

Dan started mumbling as we dragged him out the front door.

"He doesn't want to leave," I said.

Beth started laughing and fell backwards onto the front lawn. Finally, we got him to the Camaro. We opened the door, but then couldn't get him in.

"It's not going to work," I said.

"What should we do?"

"I don't know," I said. "Ask him."

Dan was lying in the grass next to the car, still mumbling to himself.

I said, "Two chickens and a coke? What?"

"What?" Beth said, laughing.

"Actually, I'm kind of hungry," I said.

Beth shrugged. "I guess we can just leave him here."

Dan rolled onto his side and started snoring.

"Yeah, he looks pretty comfortable," I said.

We drove over to Dennys. Beth ordered a Diet Coke and I ordered the full breakfast—eggs, bacon, pancakes.

"You really are hungry," Beth said.

"All that heavy lifting."

Beth smiled. She was wearing her Whitman sweatshirt and no makeup. Sitting there in the padded booth under the yellow light, she reminded me of the way that my sister's friends had looked to me when I was a kid—which is to say Beth didn't look like a high school kid anymore. I wondered what I looked like. Could we be getting older? Already?

I must have had a goofy expression on my face right then, because Beth said, "You okay?"

"Fine," I said.

When the food came, Beth took some of my bacon.

"Hey," I said. "That's rude."

"Mmmmm, bacon," Beth said.

I shielded my plate. "Better enjoy it. I'm cutting you off."

Beth laughed. "Remember when we used to come here?"

"When?"

"After I first got my license."

"I guess." I remembered that it was right around the time she had started seeing Dan. I had to hear about how exciting their sex life was. It was irritating.

"Well, here we are again."

"Here we are," I said.

Beth smiled and shook her head. "Funny."

Beth drove me back to my house. When she pulled up in front, she said "You're the guy I can always count on, you know."

"Gee, thanks."

She smiled. Then she frowned slightly and put her forehead on my shoulder. We stayed like that for several seconds. I could feel her light breath on my arm.

Then she said, "Hey?"

"Yeah?" I said.

"Do you hate me?"

"No," I said. "Why?"

"I think that I would." She lifted her head and looked at me.

I smiled, and then I couldn't help laughing—though it felt like I was laughing at myself. Like I was outside myself.

"What?" she said. "Why are you laughing?"

"I don't know."

"Well stop."

"Okay," I said. And I did.

She shook her head and turned to look out the windshield. And when she looked at me again, it was like she was thinking of something or someone else entirely.

"Well, goodnight," she said.

"Goodnight," I said.

After she drove off, I went and lay down on the hood of the Barracuda. The stars pressed up right against my face.

Twenty-five

To celebrate the sale of the house, my dad took me and Gwen and her kid to dinner. He took us to this seafood place that had just opened. All they had was fish. You could get just about any fish cooked any way you wanted, and then you had a choice of potatoes or rice, and mixed vegetables or coleslaw. The place was as big as a high school gym, and they packed people in there. The owners must have been making a killing.

The four of us sat down and my father ordered a bottle of wine. Gwen said, "Ben, put your napkin in your lap."

Ben had his fist in his water glass. He ignored her.

"Ben, put your napkin in your lap."

Ben pulled out some ice cubes and stuck them in his mouth.

Gwen sighed and put the napkin in his lap. Ben wiped his wet hands on the napkin. Then he threw it on the floor. He made a big ice-filled grin.

"Ben, do you want to go home?" Gwen said. "I'll take you home."

My father, who had been looking at the menu through all of this, cleared his throat. Gwen glared at him. She reached down and put the napkin back in Ben's lap. Ben threw it on the floor again and let out a shrill laugh.

"That's it," she said. "We're going home."

She grabbed his hand and pulled him from the table. I watched as they walked out of the restaurant.

"Is she really going to take him home?"

"I doubt it," my father said. He put down the menu and looked around, like he had only just noticed that he was in a big noisy restaurant.

"Look at all the people in here. This place is like a goddamn madhouse."

Later, after Gwen and Ben had returned, after we had eaten our fish, my father got up and went to the bathroom. Gwen said, "Have you been having a good summer?"

"Yeah," I said.

"Must be sad to see your house get torn down."

"I'm glad, actually."

"Really? Why?"

I shrugged. I didn't really feel glad, but I didn't know how else to explain it.

Gwen said, "I think I would cry."

My dad had been gone for quite some time. I excused myself.

I found him in the bathroom, looking at himself in the mirror.

"Dad, what are you doing?"

He shook his head. "I look like shit, don't I?"

"What are you talking about?"

"I look old."

"You are old."

My dad frowned.

"It's the fluorescent lights," I said.

My father glanced up at the lights, then looked back in the mirror.

"Can we get out of here?" I said.

My father turned on the tap. He started washing his hands. He said, "Gwen is pregnant."

"What?"

"She's pregnant."

"Pregnant," I said.

He nodded, pumping the soap dispenser. Then he said, "Look at this soap. It's pink."

Jack and I went over to my old house the night before they were supposed to tear the house down. The Patricks were out that night—they'd taken Sara to some church-related function—and we had started drinking Mr. Patrick's beer. Jack didn't want to be there when they got home.

My old house was empty. There were shadows on the walls where bookshelves and paintings had been, indentations in the carpet from the legs of tables and chairs. The power had been shut off, so the only light was from the moon and the streetlight outside.

Earlier that week, I had found my old wrist rocket—right where I'd hidden it in high school, wedged behind a box at the back of my closet. I'd filled my pockets with rocks and a bunch of marbles I had found in Mike's desk drawer. I'd also brought along a spark plug—ceramic was supposed to be good for safety glass.

There isn't much to shoot at in an empty house. The light bulbs made a cool popping sound, and the bathroom mirrors cracked nicely. The marbles weren't so effective as they were dramatic—shattering into a million pieces on impact. The rocks would ricochet around the room. One tagged me in the back of the leg.

Jack finished off a beer and tossed the bottle down the hallway. It skittered, then broke against the far wall. Then he said, "Let me try."

I handed him the wrist rocket.

Jack shot a few rocks at the living room window. The window flexed a bit but didn't break.

Jack said, "I ran into Simon today."

I tried to remember who Simon was. Then I remembered: he was one of Mike's old friends.

"He told me he'd seen Mike."

"What?" I said. "Where?"

"Here. Said he saw him at Mountain Man's Pizza."

I laughed. "He's working there?" Mountain Man's Pizza was this crappy pizza joint with a big-screen TV and little red candles on the tables. When we were kids, we'd held all of our soccer team parties there.

"No," Jack said. "He was eating."

"Was he sure it was him?"

"That's what I said. He said he was sure."

Jack shot another rock at the window. It bounced harmlessly off the glass.

I said, "Try this," and handed him the spark plug. Jack aimed and fired. The living room window turned white and fell away.

"Damn," Jack said.

We had to search around in the broken bits of glass in the dirt outside before we found the spark plug.

I said, "So what are you going to do?"

"About what?"

"About Mike."

Jack shrugged. "I'm not gonna go looking for him if that's what you mean."

Just then the yuppie's lights went on. We turned to see him standing by the back door in his boxer shorts. He shut the light off again.

Jack said, "Remember the guy who lived there before?"

"The guy with the Vette?"

Jack laughed. "Yeah."

Jack and I used to crank call the poor guy mercilessly. We had this good cop/bad cop routine we'd do—which was probably incomprehensible on the other end of the line. I remember laughing so hard one time that I peed my pants.

Jack said, "My dad said he saw him on TV last week, doing an infomercial."

"You think it was really him?"

"I doubt it."

"Your dad watches too much TV."

Jack laughed. "No shit."

Jack handed me the wrist rocket and I sent the spark plug through the kitchen window. After that, Jack and I were meticulous. We took out every window, one by one.

The bulldozers arrived—two of them. I'd seen demolition crews on TV, where they trigger a series of explosions, causing a large office building to sink into the ground. Sometimes there'd be a soundtrack—Beethoven or something.

The bulldozers were less elegant. They made a lot of noise and exhaust and stirred up big clouds of dust.

Mr. Patrick and I watched from across the street. He was wearing a button-up sweater and new glasses that darkened in the sunlight—he seemed very proud of them. I wondered if he noticed that the windows were gone.

I thought I'd feel more when the house came down—I thought my life would start flashing before my eyes or something like that. Instead, I just felt hungry. Dust was swirling around the place, and the bulldozers were ripping my old house apart, and all I could think about was Mrs. Patrick's famous tuna salad sandwiches.

As the last section came down—the area that had been my sister's bedroom—Mr. Patrick shook his head.

"There goes the neighborhood," he said.

Twenty-six

I stayed in Mike's room. I probably could've slept in the living room or on Jack's floor, but I didn't want to make a big deal out of it if the Patricks didn't.

Their house was a noisy place at night. The ventilation system would pick up sounds in one room and broadcast them into other rooms. And the ancient thermostat was always active, clicking on and off at odd intervals.

Often, I would watch TV with Mr. Patrick until he went to bed, and then watch a while longer until I could barely keep my eyes open. But once in bed, I would lie awake, listening: to Mr. Patrick snoring down the hall, to Sara murmuring in her sleep, to the dogs—their toenails on the hardwood floors. Mrs. Patrick got up in the middle of the night to make herbal tea—the whistle of the kettle was like a siren. And then Jack woke up at sunrise. I'd hear him running through the gears, pumping up his tires before his ride.

Mike kept showing up in my dreams. He always had this irritating smile, and he wouldn't answer my questions.

One night, I woke up suddenly. I could hear breathing in the room.

"Mike?"

I fumbled along the wall and finally switched on the light. Sara was standing there, watching me. She was wearing a full pajama bodysuit with the built-in feet.

"What are you doing?" I said.

She answered by making a clicking sound with her tongue. Jack had told me that her mother had been killed by her father, who was now in jail.

"Shouldn't you be asleep?"

At my stupid question, she went cross-eyed. Then she turned and walked out of the room.

I shut off the light. From the bed, I could just see the faint outline of Mike's little league trophies.

I fixed up the Barracuda with a new alternator, new points and spark plugs. I also got new tires and had Larry do some front end work. After that it ran like a champ.

Mrs. Patrick asked me to take Sara to the dentist. Sara was excited to discover that my car had no seatbelts. The second we got going, she started climbing all over the car. First she was on the floor, then she was in the back seat, giggling her head off.

I parked at the dentist's office. I got out and when I looked around, I saw that Sara had locked herself in the car. She was making faces at me. I shrugged and walked away. A few seconds later I heard the door slam and then she was walking right next to me. She took my hand.

It was the same dentist's office I had gone to when I was a kid. Since then, the whole place had been remodeled and painted this sick pinkish-orange color. I sat in the waiting room, reading magazines and listening to the muzak.

The half hour I sat in the waiting room kind of summed up my whole summer: here I was, bored in a pleasant but otherwise dull, artificial place that I knew and remembered, a place that was transforming into something I didn't know at all—something I didn't want to know anymore.

After a while, Sara came out with this big exaggerated grin, her pockets stuffed with dental floss and toothbrushes.

The last few weeks of summer really started to drag. I was done building bikes, Beth had gone up to Tahoe, and Jack wasn't around much—he was either at work, riding his bike, or asleep. I was pretty much just sitting around, waiting for school to start.

I got really into walking the dogs. Sara would tag along, and I'd let the dogs run off the leash—they'd smell around in people's yards, lift their legs on cars and garbage cans. Sara would lag way behind, clutching some piece of trash or something she'd stolen out of someone's yard—like a gardening tool or a Nerf football. I'd ask her to drop it or put it back and she'd just giggle.

One day I got back from walking the dogs and noticed a Toyota pickup parked across the street. I waited for Sara to go inside with the dogs. Then I crossed the street.

"Mike?" I said.

"How's it going, Colin?"

He was just sitting there, smoking a cigarette. He had lost weight—the skin was pulled tight around his features, and he was deeply tanned. His hair was long, too, sticking out around his ears from under an Oakland A's baseball cap.

"You on a stake out?" I said.

"That's right." He smiled. "Dude, they fucked up your house."

"No shit."

"I see someone fixed up my old Plymouth."

"Your dad sold it to me."

He laughed. "Why'd you want that piece of shit?"

I shrugged. "Got it running pretty good."

"For now," he said. He flicked his cigarette out the window.

Mike didn't seem like the guy I grew up with. He seemed more like a character out of some stupid movie—like an actor in a fake, contrived world. I felt like grabbing him and pulling him out of the truck—pulling him back into the real world.

I said, "How long you been back?"

"A while."

"You gonna tell your parents?"

He laughed. "What is this, twenty questions?"

I shrugged.

"I'm gonna take off. But tell Jack I'm at Kevin's. If he cares."

The "If he cares" part kind of annoyed me. I said, "Alright."

He started up the truck. "Later."

I called Jack at the shop, but he had already left for a ride. So I told him when he got home.

"Fucking asshole. He's at Kevin's?"

"Yeah. I thought Kevin was in New York or something."

"No, he dropped out of school. He's living in some shithole in East Palo Alto. I think he's dealing pot or something." He shook his head. "Fucking Mike."

East Palo Alto had briefly enjoyed some notoriety as the murder capital of the country. I think they sent in the National Guard. The place had settled down a bit after that.

Kevin's apartment was on the first floor of what looked like an old motel. It was next door to a gas station and directly across from a liquor store.

We knocked on the door—which had obviously been forced open at least once. After a moment, Kevin answered. He looked exactly like he had in high school: short, stocky, thick dark hair. He was wearing jeans and an Iron Maiden t-shirt.

"Hey Jack. Hey Colin."

"Hey Kevin," Jack said.

"Here for the fugitive?"

Jack nodded.

"I think he's taking a shit."

We walked in. Wall to wall carpet, dingy green walls. The place reeked of stale pizza and pot. The TV was tuned to Cops.

Kevin yelled, "Hey Mike. Your bro's here!" Kevin laughed. He seemed pretty stoned.

We heard the toilet flush and then Mike stepped out of the bathroom. He looked skinny as hell in his t-shirt and jeans.

Jack said, "Hi Mike."

"Jack."

There was a silence. Kevin turned to me. "You want a beer?"

"Sure," I said.

"Jack?"

Jack shook his head, no.

Kevin got me a beer out of the fridge. Then he went over and sat on the couch in front of the TV. I followed.

Kevin shoved a pile of newspapers off the couch and onto the floor. "Make yourself at home."

I sat down, cracked open my beer. We were watching Cops. Most of the episodes are about drunks, drug dealers, or domestic abuse. This episode was a pretty standard domestic abuse call—it had the usual fat drunk guy with his shirt off, cursing at the cops and cursing at his fat wife.

I glanced back at Jack and Mike, who were talking quietly over by the kitchen sink. Jack had his arms crossed. It looked like he was letting Mike do most of the talking.

I'd spent a decent amount of time thinking about Mike over the past few months, but now that we were here, I realized that I didn't care if I ever saw him again. I just felt bad for Jack. It was weird, but it was like I was already looking back on this, like I was already miles and years away.

On TV, the guy was getting wrestled to the kitchen floor and cuffed. His wife was crying.

Kevin said, "I love family drama."

I couldn't tell if he was talking about Mike or if he was talking about the show. Probably both.

On the way back, I said, "So what did you guys talk about?"

Jack shrugged. "Nothing, really." He popped open the chrome ashtray, then shut it again.

I said, "So what's he going to do?"

"Fuck if I know," he said. "He's acting like a total pussy."

"What? Still can't face your parents?"

"I guess not."

Jack turned and looked out the window. We were driving down University Avenue, passing the huge mansions just across the freeway from the trash-strewn streets of East Palo Alto.

Then Jack said, "I can't wait to get the fuck out of here."

Twenty-seven

A week before I left, my dad came by in his new Saab. He showed me the power seats, the power sunroof, the fancy stereo.

"What'd you do with the Porsche?"

"Hey, I sold the house, why not the car?"

"What?" I said. "Why'd you do that?"

"Gwen didn't like it. She thought it was dangerous."

I shook my head. My dad smiled and looked over at our old property. "Seen much activity over there?"

I shrugged.

"The realtor told me that the guy's been having some money problems."

"What do you mean?"

"I guess his loan fell through. He doesn't have the money to build the new house."

"So what's he going to do?"

My dad shrugged. "Pitch a tent?" He laughed at his joke. Then he said, "Gwen decided to get an abortion."

I stared at him for a second. "Gwen decided?"

"Well, both of us, I guess."

I looked down at a rock, lying in the gutter. I reached down and picked it up.

My father said, "So it turns out I'm going to be gone for a week or so on business. So I won't be able to see you off."

"That's cool." The rock was the size of a golf ball. It was almost perfectly round.

He smiled, then started the car. "Let me know when I can come visit you in your new place."

"Sure," I said.

"Good," he said. With that, he put it in first and pulled away.

On an impulse, I threw the rock at my father's car as it headed down the block. My stomach fluttered as it soared through the air—in my mind, I saw it hit the rear window, saw the window burst. But it fell short.

After I got another nosebleed in the Patrick's living room—getting blood on one of their nice oriental rugs—Mrs. Patrick made an appointment for me with the family doctor.

He was an old guy with a crazy comb-over. I sat on the white paper on the padded table while he dug around in one of his cabinets. Finally, he produced a small wand-type thing.

"What are you going to do with that?" I said.

"I'm going to cauterize the vein that's causing all the trouble."

I said, "Oh."

He stuck the wand up my nose. There was a clicking sound and a burning smell. He pulled out the wand.

"All set."

"That's it?" I said.

"That's it," he said. "Come back if you get another one, but you should be fixed."

"Thanks," I said.

"Just don't pick your nose."

"Okay."

"And don't do any coke."

"Right."

"And no fist fights."

"Got it."

A few days later I saw my dad's Porsche out in front of the Saab/Porsche dealership with some balloons tied to the antenna. It was all cleaned up—they'd buffed out the paint and shined up the chrome.

I pulled over, got out and walked over to the car. It was past six o'clock and the dealership was closed. No one was around.

I took out my keychain—I still had the keys. I unlocked the door and sat in the freshly vacuumed, freshly scented interior.

I wondered who would end up with it. Some yuppie who'd wash and wax it every weekend? Or maybe someone would buy it for their kid, who'd trash it in a week.

I remember when my dad came home with it—he'd bought it off a lot on the spur of the moment. My mother was furious—she wasn't working at the time, and we didn't have much money. My father pointed out that it was practical—it got good gas mileage, and look, it had two little kid-size seats in the back. But my mom stayed angry, and refused to go for a ride. So my sister and I climbed in back, and we drove around the neighborhood, that six cylinder so loud I couldn't hear what my dad was saying. But I could see how happy he was—I could see him smiling in the rear-view mirror.

The Porsche started right up. Sounded like they'd given it a tune-up, too.

At first I didn't know where I was going. I headed up to Skyline, cut down through the redwoods toward the ocean and drove north on Highway One with the sun low over the Pacific. The flat six whirred behind me. Compared to the Plymouth, driving the Porsche was like driving a go-cart—you sat on the floor and the car seemed to fit perfectly around you. It was snug and noisy and nimble feeling.

Driving along, my head seemed to clear a bit. I'd had all this crap bouncing around in there—stuff about Mike and Jack and Beth and Gordie and my dad. It was a big jumble, and I couldn't really focus on any of it—everything just kind of swirled around and I ended up with this vague, sour feeling in the bottom of my stomach. But now I just focused on the road, on the double yellow line.

I turned back up Highway 92, driving past the pumpkin farms of Half Moon Bay in the early evening light. I crossed the reservoir, and then I was on 280, heading north, toward San Francisco.

The house looked a lot like I had imagined it would—with the big gate and the circular driveway. It had a Spanish theme—white walls with a red tile roof. I rang the doorbell before I could change my mind.

Mercedes Steve answered.

"Colin? What are you doing here?"

"Well, you know... I was in the neighborhood?"

"I see." He didn't budge from the door.

"So," I said. "Get your car fixed?"

"It was totaled," he said, flatly.

"Oh, right," I said. "Hey, is Chloe around?"

Then I heard Chloe. "Who is it?" She walked up behind her brother and smiled. "Hi Colin."

We sat in the five-billion-dollar kitchen, drinking purified water. Chloe's hair was wet from having just taken a shower—spotting her light blue dress with water.

"Nice tile," I said. "Imported from Italy?"

She smiled. "Spain, actually." Then she said, "I go back to Wellesley tomorrow."

"You excited?"

"I guess." Then she said, "How's your friend?"

"Gordie?"

"Yeah."

"He's home with his mom and dad."

"But he's okay?"

"I guess."

"Some friend you are."

I shrugged.

A grandfather clock down the hall did its routine for eight o'clock.

"Let's go somewhere," I said.

"Okay."

We got into the Porsche. Chloe said, "Where'd you get this car?"

"I stole it."

She laughed.

I said, "Where to?"

"You ever been to the Sutro Baths?"

"What's that?"

"You'll see."

It was dark and foggy. You could hear the ocean but you couldn't really see it.

"Is this it?" We were looking at the concrete ruins of an old building, flooded by ocean water.

"This is it. The baths were destroyed by a fire in the 50s. Supposedly for the insurance money."

We walked down the sandy steps that led to the ocean. Some kids were sitting against the cliff, drinking. Chloe bummed a cigarette off of one of them. The kid stood up to light it for her. It was pretty windy out, so it took a while to get it lit.

"Wow, smoking. Cool."

Chloe laughed. "Shut up." We walked down closer to the water. Waves were breaking against a large rock covered with seagull shit.

She said, "I love it here."

"It's okay."

"It's way better than okay." Chloe threw away her half-smoked cigarette.

"Tobacco waster."

"Shut up."

"There are people starving for a smoke in China."

"Shut up!"

It was cold, and she huddled up to me. We started kissing, then stopped.

Chloe said, "Let's go over here."

I followed her down around the corner, then we sat under the cliff, out of the wind. We kissed some more, but mostly we just sat there, not talking, looking out at the dark water.

After a while I said, "Why do we keep ending up on cold beaches?"

"I know somewhere else we can go."

"What's this place?" She had brought me to another large house.

"It's my grandmother's house." She pulled out a key hidden in a flower pot and opened the front door.

"And where is she?"

"She's at her other house."

"In Spain?"

"No," Chloe said, laughing. "Italy."

We walked into the dark house.

"So no one's here?" I said.

"Just us."

"Spooky."

"Scared?" Chloe said.

"Very scared."

We ended up having sex—well, something that approximated sex, since we didn't have a condom—on an expensive couch that was very uncomfortable. Then, after a while, we both fell asleep.

When I woke up, at first, I didn't know where I was. Then I heard the foghorn and remembered.

Chloe's hair splayed out along her shoulder, parting in one place to reveal a light indentation from an old TB vaccination. When I touched her, she shivered and sat up. "What time is it?"

"I don't know."

Just then, another grandfather clock did its thing—ringing three times.

"Three," I said.

Chloe said, "Shit, I should get home." She got up off the couch, scooped her clothes off the floor and tip-toed out of the room.

While she was in the bathroom, I got dressed. Then I walked around the living room, looking at the fancy rugs, fancy furniture, fancy knick-knacks on the fancy mantelpiece. It was like a museum. I looked out the window and saw my dad's old Porsche parked out front. The front windshield was wet with mist. Somehow, none of this seemed real to me.

Chloe walked out of the bathroom, running a comb through her hair. She smiled. "Ready?"

"Ready."

It was just starting to get light by the time I got back to the car lot. All the other cars were covered with dew, shining in the glare of the streetlight. I parked the Porsche where I had found it, then sat there a second.

I thought about Chloe, how I would probably never see her again. I would probably never see this car again. I would never see this stretch of El Camino in this exact light again, either. I wasn't sure that I cared, either. It was just a moment—just me passing through time.

I took the Porsche's cigarette lighter and put it in my pocket.

It took a while to get the Barracuda started, but finally the engine caught. I warmed it up, then pulled out into the empty street, all the stoplights flashing yellow.

Twenty-eight

Beth dropped by the day before I left. She didn't want to come into the Patricks' house. (A few years before, Beth had said some stuff in front of Mrs. Patrick when she was drunk. I don't remember what exactly—it wasn't a big deal, and she had apologized. But she was still nervous around Mrs. Patrick.) So I came outside and we walked across the street to the site of my old house. The new lawn was covered with Caterpillar tread marks, and there was a shallow hole where the house used to be.

"Weird," she said.

"Yeah."

"You think if we come back in twenty years we'll recognize anything?"

I shrugged. "Who knows."

A car drove past. It blew through the stop sign that had been put in the week before.

Beth was wearing new Keds. They were bright white. "New shoes?"

"New shoes for school," she said, and laughed. "Like 'em?"

"Very nice."

When I tried to step on one of them, Beth squealed and jumped back. "Quit it!"

I smiled.

"Well," she said. "Tell Pablo he's a shit."

I laughed. "I will."

"You're a shit, too."

"What do you mean?"

"All boys are shits."

"Isn't that a bit of a generalization?"

"True though."

I looked down at the ground—at a twisted piece of aluminum. I bent down and picked it up. It was something from the house, maybe a window frame.

She smiled. "Okay, you're not a shit."

I was looking at that bent piece of aluminum and guess I kind of spaced out for a second. Then I saw that Beth was looking at me with a goofy grin on her face.

"What?" I said.

"You're funny."

"I'm funny?"

"Yeah."

I shook my head. I realized that the piece of aluminum was part of my old shower stall—part of the frame that kept the Plexiglas door on track. Once, when I was a kid, I slipped on the bathmat and fell right on it—splitting my chin open.

Beth said, "I should go. I'm late for work."

"Alright."

She gave me a kiss on the cheek.

"Bye Colin."

"Bye," I said. I watched her drive away in that little Subaru. Then I turned and tossed the piece of aluminum over the yuppie's fence.

I was still standing out there when a Honda pulled up in front of the old widow's house. A middle-aged man got out, who I recognized as the widow's son—or son-in-law—I was never sure.

He went around to the back of the car and opened the hatchback, revealing a giant TV. He saw me and nodded.

"How's it going?" I said.

"Alright. What happened to your house?"

"Freak tornado."

"Pretty localized."

He started tugging on the TV.

"Need help?"

"That would be great."

I walked over.

"We just got a new one. I thought I'd give this to my mom. She's had the same black and white forever."

We got it out and walked sideways up the front walk. He got the screen door open with one hand and knocked.

No answer.

"Mom! It's me!"

Just as I was thinking: maybe she's dead, the door opened. His mother was in her usual bathrobe.

"Oh," she said. "I'll get out of your way."

It took my eyes a second to adjust to the darkness inside—she had the shades drawn. I almost tripped on a rug in the hallway.

We brought the TV into the living room and set it down on the coffee table—crushing my fingers. The guy moved the tiny black and white off the small folding table and set it on the floor. Then we put the color in its place. The little table seemed like it was about to buckle.

"There you go," he said, and handed her the remote.

"What's this?"

"It's the remote."

"Let me get my glasses."

She walked into the dining room.

I looked around. The place was cluttered as hell. There were National Geographics all over the place. I picked up one of them: 1956. Naked Africans rowing a boat. I put the magazine back down. I'd lived next door all my life and I think this was first time I'd been inside.

Mrs. Greer came back with her glasses on. Then I saw what I had somehow missed before: her hair was down. Normally it was up in a bun. But now it was down. Long gray hair past her waist.

She picked up the remote and frowned. Then she handed it back to her son. "I'll just lose it, anyway."

"Mom." He took it from her and switched on the TV. "See, it's easy."

She looked at me. "Would you like something to drink?"

"Sure," I said.

After his mother disappeared again, he said, "Depressing, isn't it?"

"What?"

He motioned vaguely around the room. "This."

I shrugged. "I don't know."

"We keep trying to get her to move into a retirement home, but she refuses."

"I don't blame her."

Mrs. Greer came back with two glasses filled with red liquid. She handed us each one.

Her son said, "Cheers," and took a drink. I did, too. It took me a second to figure out what it was—Hawaiian Punch, with ice cubes that tasted like they'd been in a freezer for a while.

"Taste okay?" Mrs. Greer said.

"Great," I said.

My mother called later that afternoon. Mrs. Patrick answered, and they exchanged the necessary pleasantries. The two of them had never really been friends—my mom wasn't into church, wasn't into the whole housewife thing.

Mrs. Patrick left the phone on the kitchen counter and went outside with her pruning scissors. I picked up the phone.

"I talked to your father. He told me about the house."

"All gone," I said.

"I always liked that house."

I had to laugh at that one. I couldn't help it.

Then she said, "I'm sending you a check."

"What?" I said. "Why?"

"For school. You are going back, aren't you?"

"Yeah," I said.

"Good."

I hated money stuff. There was some significance in the fact that my mother was sending me the check. I knew there was some kind of weird power struggle going on between my parents, but I didn't really want to know about it.

"I'm so glad you could come out to Arizona this summer. We have to start planning your next visit."

"Okay," I said. Outside, Mrs. Patrick was pruning one of the oleander bushes, collecting the clippings in a small wicker basket.

"Maybe you could come out for Thanksgiving."

"Maybe."

"Well, you let me know what works for you."

"Okay, Mom."

"I love you."

"I love you, too."

After my mom called, I sat around for a while, eating an apple and looking out across at our old property. I still wasn't used to the view. You could see clear across to our back fence. I kept thinking I'd blink and our house would pop back up like a Hollywood prop.

Then I thought of something. I took the phone and dialed our old number. We'd had that number as long as I could remember. I'd memorized it when I was a little kid and would probably remember it the rest of my life: 326-2697. So I dialed. It rang once and then a scratchy recorded voice came on. "We're sorry, your call cannot be completed as dialed. The number has been disconnected. Please check the number and dial again."

I hung up. Of course, I had known that would happen. But I had also hoped that maybe someone would pick up. Dialing had felt weird, like I was reaching out, reaching back into the Twilight Zone. I wondered who would get the new number. Right now, it was in limbo—like my dad's Porsche—waiting to be passed on to someone else.

And then I remembered our dorm room phone. Gordie and I had never disconnected it. It took me a second to remember the number, and then I dialed.

I half expected Gordie to answer, but it just kept ringing. So it was still hooked up. I wondered if the phone company would track us down, try to make us pay for someone's phone sex calls, or the long-distance calls of some foreign student.

I was about to hang up when someone answered, out of breath. "Hello?"

"Hello?" I said.

"Yes?"

"Who's this?"

"Who is this?"

"You're in my old room," I said. "You're on my phone."

"Excuse me?"

"I said you're talking on my phone."

"I don't know what you're talking about."

"I used to live in that room. I never disconnected the phone."

The guy seemed to be thinking about this. I said, "Are you in summer school or something?"

"No, I just moved in. I plugged in the phone and it worked."

"Well don't use it."

"What do you mean? It's my phone."

I said, "No, it's my phone." But I wasn't even thinking about the phone anymore. I was thinking about the new guy in my old room. He was probably wearing a brand new Cal sweatshirt, probably thought the girl next door was cute. And I was jealous of him, jealous of how life must seem new to him right then—everything new and full of possibility.

The guy said, "I'm hanging up." And what do you know? He hung up.

Mr. Patrick walked in and opened the refrigerator. "We out of peanut butter again?"

"I think there's some in the door."

"Oh yeah," he said. "Thanks."

I spent a few hours packing my stuff. Pablo had found us some cheap dump in Oakland. As soon as I got there I was going to have to find a bed and bedding and other junk, but I wasn't going to worry about that now. I just didn't want to take or keep a bunch of crap I would never use.

I gave Sara my old football video game along with my sister's *Charlie's Angels* lunchbox and Squirrel. I also gave her Gordie's stupid trophy. I kept Dan's buck knife, the Porsche's cigarette lighter and the little Civil War soldier the old guy had given me in the bar. Pretty much everything else that I hadn't already thrown away I put in the trunk of the car.

After that, I was bored. I drove over to Safeway. I was in the checkout line when who walks up behind me but Dan.

"Let me ask you one question," he said. He was holding a six-pack of Molson. He always drank Canadian beer. I couldn't figure that out.

"Alright," I said.

"Are you fucking Beth?"

"What?" I said.

"You are, aren't you?"

The belt started moving, pulling my Coke toward the cashier.

"No," I said.

"Cause I don't give a fuck. You can do whatever you want with that bitch."

We stared at each other for a long second. Then Dan picked up the little divider stick thing and put it down on the belt.

I paid for my Coke and got out of there.

Then, in the parking lot. "Hey Colin?"

I turned around to see Dan running up to me. This was it. I put my Coke down on the hood of the Barracuda, ready to fight.

"Hey," he said, stopping to catch his breath. "Can I borrow five bucks?"

It took me a second to process what he had said.

"I'll pay you back," he said.

I wanted to laugh. I opened my wallet, pulled out a five and handed it to him.

Dan smiled. "You're alright, Colin." And then he walked away, shaking his head and laughing.

That night, Jack and I stayed up drinking at the school. We sat out on the blacktop. I'd brought the wrist rocket along, and we took turns taking pot shots at a nearby transformer box.

After a while Jack said, "I think I'm gonna go early."

At first I didn't know what he was talking about, but then I realized he was talking about Europe.

He continued: "I mean, I might as well get used to riding in the rain."

I nodded.

"I've got the money saved up. And I met some guy who knows a place I can stay for a while."

"You should do it," I said.

"Yeah. I think I'm gonna. Maybe September."

"How's your French?"

"Muy bien."

I smiled and shook my head. Jack wasn't gone yet but he was gone: I could see him in Belgium on a rainy training ride, his jersey splattered up the back with Belgian mud.

Then I said, "Heard anything from Mike?"

"He came by the shop yesterday."

"Yeah?"

Jack shrugged. "Typical Mike bullshit. Said he was going to move out to New York with Kevin."

"I thought you said Kevin had dropped out."

Jack shrugged. "I guess not."

"And your parents still know nothing?"

Jack shook his head. "Nope. And I'm staying out of it."

Jack let fly a large rock. It hit the transformer box with a BLAM! The box started shooting sparks, lighting up the night.

"Oh shit!" Jack said. We jumped up and started running. Running and laughing.

Jack went to bed but I was still wide awake. I started walking. Somehow, I ended up over at the pool.

I found a tall tree next to the fence, climbed it, and dropped onto the soft grass on the other side.

The water was completely smooth. And it was quiet—there was only the dull hum of the pumps. I knelt next to the pool and felt the water. It was warm compared to the night air, and I could smell the chlorine.

As I pulled off my shirt and then my pants, I thought about that night at the pool with Gordie and Beth. And then I remembered those hippies at Berkeley, running around naked in the sprinklers. It seemed like an incredibly long time ago.

I stripped down the rest of the way. Then, not wanting to disturb the glass-like surface, I slipped in over the side. I pushed off the wall and let myself float into the middle of the pool.

I put my feet down in the middle and then I just stood there, feeling the contrast between the slick lane line and the rough pool bottom. The water clung lightly to my shoulders and I could feel the soft pulse of the wake my movement had caused.

I thought of everything that had happened that summer. I felt bad about Gordie, but he seemed far away now. So did my father, so did Jack and Beth and Mike and Chloe.

Still, I couldn't help thinking that I'd failed Gordie somehow. But then I didn't know what I would've done differently.

What about Jack? And what about my dad? Had I failed them, too?

But what can you really do for a person anyway? At some point everyone pulls back. Jack pulled back from Mike. My mom had pulled back from my dad. When you get down to it, everyone is alone. Eventually, everyone ends up like that old widow. Like my mom said, worry about yourself.

And then I started thinking about this movie they showed us in kindergarten—I think it was called "Paddle to the Sea." It started with some Indian guy carving a little wooden boat with a little wooden Indian guy in it. He did a nice job—he painted it and everything. Then he marched up into the mountains and planted it in the snow. The little boat just sat there for a while. But then spring came and the snow started to melt. After a while, the boat started moving, slowly at first, just kind of slip sliding down the hillside. Pretty soon the boat found its way into a small stream, which turned into a bigger stream, which turned into violent, churning rapids. After a while, the rapids spilled out into the sea.

I remember that I really identified with that wooden Indian in that little boat. I mean, you're just sitting there, minding your own business, and then shit starts breaking down under you. And then you're moving, faster and faster, just trying to hold on. But if you hold on, eventually you'll make it to the ocean. I can't remember what happened with the wooden Indian once he got there. Maybe nothing. Maybe he just floated around for a while.

So now summer was over and I felt like I'd just spilled out into the ocean. It was up to me to decide what to do next.

The wind moved through the trees overhead, making a rushing sound. I looked out across the still surface of the pool and knew I wasn't ever coming back—not really, anyway. I was done with this place.

After a while, I got out of the pool. I pulled my clothes on over and climbed back over the fence.

I woke up early—six o'clock. The air was cold as I put my last things into the car.

The Patricks came outside to see me off, like they were my real parents. Sara came out, too. A few days before, she'd stolen an orange hula hoop out of someone's yard— one of those ones with the ball bearings that rattle around the inside. She was still getting the hang of it. It kept clattering onto the sidewalk.

The Barracuda felt solid and heavy with the weight of the boxes as I got in and closed the door. Mrs. Patrick gave me a kiss through the window. Mr. Patrick wished me luck.

And that's when I remembered about owing Mr. Patrick a dollar for the Barracuda. When I handed it to him, he smiled, folded it up and put it in his pocket.

Mountain View was quiet as I drove away. Houses and lawns and hedges slid past, and there was a steady beat of air pressure and engine noise as I passed long rows of parked cars.

I merged onto 101, and the traffic increased steadily as I approached San Francisco. Then I was on the Bay Bridge— on the lower deck, in the dark. But when I came off the other side, everything opened up—no real view or anything, just concrete, blue sky and the hot California sun.